The Cursed Tower

The Mageborn Saga, Volume 2

Dayne Edmondson

Published by Dark Star Publishing, 2018.

THE CURSED TOWER

First edition. May 13, 2018.

Copyright © 2018 Dayne Edmondson.

ISBN: 978-0998426365

Written by Dayne Edmondson.

Also by Dayne Edmondson

The Dark Tide Trilogy
Emergence
Eclipse
Ruin

The Mageborn Saga
Mageborn
The Cursed Tower
Halls of Light

The Seven Stars Universe
Ghost Ranger
Space Commando

The Shadow Trilogy
Blood and Shadows
Time of Shadows
Shadows Fall

Standalone
The Complete Dark Tide Trilogy
The Complete Shadow Trilogy

Table of Contents

Thank you to my typo hunters:

Richard

Chapter 1

The Tower of the Seven Stars. A behemoth composed of black stone or metal, it dwarfed the buildings of the city of Tar Ebon. Emma craned her neck as she walked, squinting against the mid-day sun gleaming off its shimmering surface to see the top. What adventures, what mysteries, awaited them there?

Favio belched, shaking Emma from her reverie.

She gave the bard a glare she would give her brother if he did the same, eyebrow raised. He may have looked to be her father's age, but he acted much younger.

"What?" Favio said, shrugging. "Better out than in."

Emma shook her head. "Disgusting."

"You haven't spent much time among pigs then, have you?" Richard said.

"No, I haven't." *Though I've smelled some ripe people coming into Father's store.* Their store had been situated far from the markets, and the smells from her mother's shop would have overpowered the smell of livestock anyway.

The group continued in silence for a time as the tail end of the Iron Legion entered the eastern gate of Tar Ebon, making room for the mages who had gone to battle to enter. Emma walked at the end of the procession with Alivia and her companions.

"Why can't we be at the front of the mages?" Ethan asked. "You're an arch mage, right?"

Alivia offered a bemused smile. "I am an arch mage, but so are many of them." She pointed to the row in front of her. "And *you* are students. Prospective students," she corrected. "Decorum demands you walk at the rear."

1

"How are you faring?" Emma asked Kylie, ignoring her brother's grumbled response.

The girl jerked her eyes away from the Tower and met Emma's. "It's... a bit overwhelming." She sighed. "I heard stories about this place, back at the coven. My mother..." she stopped, and tears welled up in her eyes. "My mother told me one day we might visit."

The lies parents tell their children. Emma guessed Kylie's mother never had the intention of taking her, but she didn't have the heart to say that to the girl still mourning the loss of her mother days earlier.

The line moved quick and soon they were past the gates and walking on one of the main thoroughfares. Villagers who had stopped to watch the procession of the army lost interest by the time Emma and her group passed and soon they were elbowing villagers going about their business away from them. Emma had to admit there wasn't anything about her appearance which suggested she was a mage. For all the townsfolk knew she was a wash woman.

Tar Ebon reminded her of Ironforge, only more diverse. Instead of neat rows of houses of a similar design, the city boasted a wide variety of architectures sitting in clusters. The outermost houses they passed possessed straw or wooden roofs and wooden siding, while the closer they came to the center of the city the sturdier the buildings became, culminating in black stone buildings with red tile roofs. The people of Tar Ebon also wore much more flamboyant clothing than the reserved people of Ironforge. The somewhat warmer climate allowed for a wider variety of styles from tunics to dresses, robes to sleeveless shirts. Winter was a distant threat to the city.

A myriad array of smells assailed her nose as they passed bakeries, blacksmith shops, tanners, fish vendors and more. The smell of human waste, something she'd partially forgotten the smell of while traveling in the wilds, was surprisingly not as prevalent as expected for a city of this size.

"The streets smell clean," Ethan commented, speaking Emma's thought, though their neural link wasn't open at that moment. "Relatively."

"Tar Ebon prides itself on being at the forefront of sanitation," Alivia explained. "Running water and a sewer system help ensure waste doesn't get thrown out on the street."

And we thought Ironforge was advanced with our heating systems, Emma thought. Their city had nothing like this.

The army had broken off several streets back. Alivia told her they were housed in barracks throughout the city, so in the event of an attack they would be able to respond to whichever section of the city needed support the most. That made sense, considering the massive size of Tar Ebon.

Despite having rested while the army fought at Senegal Fortress, Emma's feet were burning by the time the stone houses gave way to a black inner wall surrounding the courtyard belonging to the Tower. The wall looked to be composed of the same material as the outer wall of the city, and maybe the Tower; she wasn't close enough to see yet, a stone of an impossibly black color with no visible seams. A pair of black iron gates stood open, admitting the mages inside.

"Alas, this is where I take my leave," Favio said. He bowed with a flourish of his cloak. "Ladies. Gentlemen. It's been fun."

Emma couldn't help but smile sadly at the departure of their companion who had become their eccentric friend. Sure, he had lied about his identity, but he'd been given plenty of chances to leave them in the dust and had stuck by them. Besides, Alivia trusted him.

Indeed, Alivia gave him a hug and kissed him on the cheek. "Goodbye old friend. Will you be going far?"

"That would be telling," the bard replied. "But I shall disclose this - I will be around when the time comes that you need me."

"Cryptic as always," the arch mage replied. "And if we never need you?"

"Oh, you will. I promise you that."

"A seer *and* a bard," Ethan grumbled to Richard. The farmer-turned-mage grunted in reply.

"If... if you get up to Ironforge," Emma asked, stepping forward. "Will you seek out our parents and tell them we've made it?" She fumbled around for paper before remembering they'd left most of their possessions behind at Senegal Fortress and she hadn't had paper to begin with.

Favio, seeming to read her mind, bowed again. "Of course, dear princess. Life is a wandering road, you never know where it might take you."

Emma cheeks warmed. "I'm hardly a princess."

"Every daughter is a princess in her father's eyes, my dear." He winked before shaking hands with Richard and Ethan in turn. "Take care of these lovely ladies, men." He pointed a finger at them. "But don't treat them like porcelain dolls either."

"What's a porcelain doll?" Richard asked.

"Glass," Emma said absentmindedly, remembering the doll collection her mother had. She had seemed overly fond of the dolls, going so far as whipping Ethan with one of their father's belts when he accidentally broke one.

"Indeed." Favio backed away and waved once more before disappearing into the crowd moments later. Emma didn't think the man had magic, but he certainly knew how to escape unnoticed.

The reddish cobblestones of the main thoroughfare gave way to smooth, seamless black stone. She finally had to ask. "What causes the stone to look black and have no seams?"

Alivia looked down, as if seeing their path for the first time, then looked up and smiled. "I don't notice the difference any more. But it is mage-forged stone. You'll learn more about it at the Tower, but the basic answer is that the elements of existence in each piece of stone were melded together to form a single block."

"What purpose does it serve, other than to look pretty?"

"There are many tactical reasons. First, it's much stronger than stone alone. Normal stone walls are held together by mortar, a sticky substance that hardens. But when a stone is mage-forged, the stones act as if they are forged of a single slab of stone, making the structure, or ground, much stronger."

"Nice," Ethan commented.

"The buildings in our coven were like this. But they were not black," Kylie said.

"The stronger the bond, meaning the closer the elements of existence are to one another, the darker the color because more light is absorbed." She smiled apologetically. "But you will learn all this in school. Follow me."

The courtyard bustled with activity as most of the mages entered through a wide entrance into the Tower. Emma squinted. There were no doors swung outward, and no hinges showing them swung inward. How did they... she jumped back as slabs of metal, she could tell from the glare of the sunlight on them, slid in place after a group entered and no more were coming up the ramp. *An automated door?*

Yes, it is a sliding door mechanism that uses sensors to detect movement and actuate the motors that trigger the door to...

Hold on, Emma barked to Shadow, her "Neurological Interface Assistant" or NIA for short. I don't understand half those terms. But I can see what the result is. The doors open when people approach. Is that right?

That is a highly simplistic explanation, but it is accurate.

That's all I needed. And I didn't ask you.

I shall endeavor to better detect when your inquiries are directed at me or your subconscious.

Uh, thanks, I guess.

Shadow wisely refrained from responding.

Emma studied the Tower from several yards away. It reflected the light, similar to the doors... was the Tower made of metal? Alivia had already answered one of her naïve questions and asking Shadow would likely give her a ten-minute explanation on terms she didn't yet understand, so Emma refrained from speaking, or calling upon the assistant in her head, again.

The group did not go up the ramp, depriving Emma of a chance to see the automatic doors in action. Instead, Alivia led them to a squat, square building that sat to the north of the Tower. Like the Tower, the building was black, though unlike the Tower the building looked to be made of stone. Instead she followed the others through a pair of plain wooden doors, doors flanked by two guards in blue armor, into a tall, cavernous room.

Four pillars supported the building, stretching up into shadows. A hearth burned along the left and right walls and torches filled in the gaps with light. At the far end of the building sat a chair. An empty chair, and an odd-looking chair at that. As the group neared, Emma could make out that it was made of metal, though not black metal like she suspected the Tower was made of. Suspended above the chair, attached by a bent metal rod of some sort, was a metal helmet. She opened her mouth to voice a question, but Ethan beat her to it.

"What is that?" her brother asked.

"The Sorting Chair." Alivia said.

"The what?" Kylie blurted, the first time she'd directly addressed the arch mage since waking earlier that day.

"It is used to sort students into their appropriate house," Alivia explained. "Th houses began twenty years ago, after the war against the Krai'kesh decimated our ranks." She cleared her throat as if choking down old memories. "The houses were a way to begin to specialize the new mages coming to the Tower. A division of labor to prepare us for the future."

What future? Emma wondered, thankful Shadow didn't blurt out his opinion.

"So, what, some mages are farmers?" Richard asked sarcastically.

"Agriculture is an important school of study for the survival and growth of the human race," Alivia replied.

"You can't be serious," Ethan said. "There are mages studying how to make better potatoes?"

"Among other things in nature, yes."

"Look at me, I'll be the lumberjack mage." Her brother swung his arms in a motion as though he were swinging an axe.

"Like father, like son," Alivia mumbled. Emma found herself silently agreeing.

"So, what does the Sorting Chair do?" Emma asked, trying to bring the conversation back to the matter at hand. She'd obviously brought them here for something, and the guards at the door suggested the Chair had *some* value.

"You sit in the chair and put the helmet on. You are... tested... by the chair and it determines what the best house is for you."

"So, the chair decides if I'm going to be a farmer?" Ethan asked. "What if I want to be a warrior?" He held his fist up to imitate holding a sword.

"There is a house for those bravest among the order. Many go on to become battle mages or mage guards. But we won't know until you sit in the chair."

"Is the word of this chair binding?" Kylie asked. "It cannot be changed?"

"The chair gives two choices. The mage chooses one now and may begin studying the other in a year."

"How are we tested?" Richard asked.

Alivia shook her head. "No one remembers the tests, but we know it does test us, for time passes for those watching."

"So, the chair is magical?" Emma asked.

"Of a sort," Alivia replied cryptically. "It is an ancient technology, like a sort of magic to those who do not understand it, dating back to the days of the Founders."

"Will it hurt us?" Kylie asked.

Alivia smiled kindly at the witch. "I do not think so. It has never physically harmed a student and, although students have broken into tears during the testing, they have not remembered what caused them to cry, which suggests no lasting harm."

"So, who gets to go first?" Ethan asked, in a tone that suggested false bravado. Like the time he'd asked that same question from atop their roof in Ironforge.

"I was hoping for a volunteer," Alivia said.

"I'll go first," Richard said, stepping forward and puffing his chest up. Was he trying to show off?

Alivia nodded and gestured to the chair. "Please, sit."

Richard approached the chair and sat. He placed his arms on the arms of the chair and Alivia secured them with bands of metal. He looked from Kylie to Emma and back. He *was* trying to show off. To look like he was the bravest.

Emma opened her mouth to tell him he didn't need to prove he was brave, but fear of her own crept up and stopped her. Instead she gave him a thumbs up and smiled.

Alivia lowered the helmet on his head. It covered his head like an empty bowl upended atop it. She stepped back, and a band of red light spread around the rim of the helmet.

At first, nothing happened. Then Richard shuddered, his back slamming against the chair and his hands clenching into fists. He emitted a bestial roar next, causing Emma to jump in surprise. "No, no, no," he slurred. "Not her." Tears ran down his face. He was sobbing.

"Get him out," Emma blurted, stepping toward the chair.

Alivia held out a cautionary hand. "This is part of the test. It's normal."

"It's torture!" Emma shouted. "How can you condone this?" She pointed toward her friend.

"Because he won't remember it," Alivia replied calmly.

Emma watched as the shuddering died down, though now the boy was muttering. Then the shuddering resumed until he finally sagged in relief some minutes later. The red light on the helmet morphed to blue and the metal bars restraining his arms released on their own. He raised his hands to the helmet and pushed it up, then blinked and squinted at the others. "Did I pass?"

The chair emitted a chirping sound and two pieces of paper slid out of its side and fell to the floor. Alivia picked them up. "House Arreat and House Longclaw," she announced.

"What do those mean?" Kylie asked.

"How many houses are there?" Emma asked.

"Dude, you cried like a girl," Ethan said to Richard.

"Shut up." Richard wiped the tears from his cheeks. "I don't remember anything from after she put the helmet on my head, okay?"

"House Arreat is one of the two disciplines focusing on earth magic. It involves metalworking and manipulation of the minerals and rocks of the world," Alivia explained. "They are builders. House Longclaw is a fire discipline focused on martial prowess and weapons, mundane and magical. Warfare. And to answer your question, Emma, there are seven houses."

"Of course there are," Ethan remarked. "Tower of the Seven Stars, seven houses, what's next, seven privies?"

Alivia ignored his snark and looked instead to Richard. "You must select one house."

Richard chewed his cheek as he thought. He remained seated in the chair. "House Arreat."

Alivia nodded. "It is decided. You may pursue study of the Longclaw discipline after a year, but you will forever remain a member of House Arreat."

Richard stood. "You gonna go next, Ethan, so I can see you cry?"

Ethan folded his arms. "I'm a gentleman. Ladies first."

Emma rolled her eyes and resisted the urge to punch him in the shoulder. "Fine, I'll go."

"No, I should," Kylie interrupted, stepping in front of Emma and turning to face her. "You've done so much for me, it's only right that I..."

"It's not a life and death matter," Emma argued. "The order doesn't matter." She lowered her voice and offered a smile. "But I appreciate the sentiment."

Kylie nodded slowly and stepped aside.

Emma approached the chair and sat. Like before, Alivia restrained her wrists and moved to lower the helmet down. "Do not be afraid," she said.

"I won't," Emma said, surprising herself that she meant it. She'd faced far more dangerous things than a chair. What was the worst that could happen?

The helmet descended and darkness with it. A low hum began from behind and an instant later her vision was filled with a blinding white light.

Chapter 2

E mma raced through the forest. She winced as she brushed a thorn bush, causing a cut on her forearm. Her chest heaved as she ignored the pain and leapt over a log. A vicious roar from behind shook the surrounding leaves. She had to keep going, though she didn't know why. *It will kill me*, she thought, though she couldn't remember what "it" was. Still she ran. *Run* was the sole thought in her mind, an overriding thought disallowing any other thoughts to intrude for long.

The forest ended abruptly, as if the land were sliced by a knife. Before her lay an arena. Without thought she ran onto the gritty sand, then turned around. The forest was gone, replaced by a brick wall. *What forest?* She held a sword in one hand and a shield in the other, though she couldn't remember how they came to be there. Something wasn't right, but she couldn't put her finger on it. It was like trying to hold a fish, a lesson she'd learned the one time her father took she and Ethan fishing near Ironforge. The memory of that day when she'd caught a fish and tried snatching it disappeared as quick as it came, replaced with fear once more as the *thing* approached from behind a large wooden door on the other side of the arena. The door shattered, sending splinters flying across the arena. Emma raised her shield and both felt and heard the impact of shards against it.

She lowered the shield and beheld a monster. The creature with red skin, standing twice as tall as her brother, stood on two hoofed feet, had the torso and arms of a man and the head of a bull, with horns arcing out and pointed skyward. It held a double-bladed axe in its massive hands. It threw back its head and bellowed, causing the arena to shake. Emma quivered in fear, her hands threatening to drop the sword and shield. How could she stand against such a thing?

Use magic, a voice in her head said. Magic? She didn't possess magic. No, all she had were mundane weapons. She was going to die. It would all be for nothing. Her family would... did she have a family? She couldn't remember.

The bull-man interrupted her ruminations by pawing at the ground, lowering its head and charging. Dust streamed behind him and he raised his axe as he ran.

Emma raised her shield, preparing for a strike. Wait, she, a sixteen-year-old girl, couldn't stand against a blow from such a beast. What was she thinking? She tossed the shield aside and ran toward the monster. Something inside told her the best chance for survival was to be faster than the beast. When she was a few feet away her opponent swung his axe. She changed her speed and dodged the strike, coming up behind it. She slashed at his calf and the sword hit home, slicing through flesh and hitting bone.

The creature roared in anger and limped, turning toward her. It took a step and stumbled before catching itself. But its axe slipped from its grip and slid to the ground. It struggled to take another step but roared in pain and collapsed under its weight.

Emma stepped forward cautiously and kicked the axe behind her. Then she crept further toward the man-bull and raised her sword. Now was the moment. *No,* a voice said in the back of her mind. *A mage is merciful.*

I'm not a mage! She shouted back in her mind. Here she was, arguing with herself about morality. Where had she gotten such a delusion from?

Still, she didn't lower the sword. It shook in her hands as her mind said thrust and her body refused. She blinked and studied her opponent.

The creature moaned in pain, its ferocity gone. But it would have had no qualms about murdering her. Wait, what was that? She leaned closer, holding the sword to the side. A collar around its neck. Was it a slave? Perhaps it was attacking her at its master's command. She bit her lip and raised the sword again. She slammed it down. Clang, the iron shattered, and the collar fell in pieces to the ground.

Shocked expression on its face, the creature looked up at her. It groaned in a different tone, one reminiscent of a question. "Why?" The tone seemed to ask.

"Because you are not my enemy," she said, casting the sword aside and feeling braver than she ever recalled being, which wasn't saying much.

She turned around, intending to walk away.

The landscape changed. She stood before a golden door. She turned again but the sand and the monster were gone. Had they ever really been there?

"Ah, a visitor," a voice came from behind.

Emma spun to find a giant golden cat of some sort sitting in front of her. Its green eyes studied Emma. "What are you?" She asked, tensing and wishing she possessed a weapon. Hadn't she had one? She put a hand to her head. It was so difficult to remember.

"I am the Sphinx," it replied.

"Why are you here?"

"To test you, child. Answer my riddle correctly and you may choose a door. Answer it incorrectly and you shall face death."

"Death from what?" Emma asked. She didn't see anything around.

"Why, from me, my dear." The Sphinx stretched and opened its mouth wide, revealing two rows of jagged, sharp teeth. "Are you ready?"

Emma swallowed. She didn't have a choice. "Yes."

"This thing of all things destroys, implacable. Creatures of sea and sky, of land and star. Chews iron, shreds steel. Pummels hard stone to dust. Kills kings, buries towns, and grinds mountains down. What is it?"

"How many tries do I get?"

"Three."

Emma thought hard. "Water." A flood could kill many things. The Bible told of a worldwide flood.

"Wrong," the Sphinx said, rising to its feet. "Water cannot affect the stars or creatures of the sea."

Emma took a step back. "Magic." She didn't believe in magic, but the thought just came to her.

"Wrong again." The Sphinx took steps toward her until its maw was inches away from Emma's face. "One more and you become my supper."

Think, Emma, think. Wind, earth, fire? No. A monster? Man?

Fear settled in her heart. She didn't want to die, didn't want to leave her family. What family? Did she have a family?

No, this won't be the end, she told herself. An image drifted into her mind's eye. A clock, with its arms spinning around, ticking as it told time. That was it! "Time!" She blurted out.

The Sphinx bared its teeth...in a smile. "Correct. You may enter." He stepped to the side.

Emma, casting a sideways glance at the Sphinx as she passed, placed her hand on the door knob and opened the door. She stepped through and stood on a black metal platform. She spun but the golden door was gone. And so was...whatever had been behind it. She closed her eyes, trying to hold onto the fragments of memories but they slid away.

"Emma," her father's voice called. She turned to find him tied to a stake, a pyre of wood surrounding him. Opposite him, her mother stood tied to an identical stake. A figure in a black hood stood between them, torch in hand.

"What is this?" Emma asked. "How did you get here?" she asked her parents.

"You must choose which of us to save, Emma," her mother said. Panic laced her voice, like when Emma and her brother...wait, what brother? She didn't have a brother. Like when she'd come face to face with a snake and her mother had come out to tell her to back away slowly and make no sudden movements.

Tears welled up in Emma's eyes. She couldn't choose between her parents. That was an impossible choice. *There is always a choice*, a voice echoed in her head. A memory, of her father, telling her there was always a choice, no matter how difficult. More than that, there was always a *right* choice. She blinked away the tears, refusing to show weakness by wiping them. Instead she puffed up her chest and approached the hooded figure. She could not tell whether the person was male or female as the flames growing out from the torch licked the air, hungry for something to consume.

Do the unexpected, the voice in her mind said. *Do what your opponent will least expect.* "I volunteer to take both their places."

"No!" her mother screamed.

"You can't do that!" her father shouted.

"Yes, I can." She kept her eyes locked on the darkness hiding the figure's face. "Can't I?"

The hooded figure stood still, not moving their head.

"I'll take that as a yes." She walked past the figure and a third pyre materialized beyond her parents' pyres. The wind stood still, a silent witness to her sacrifice. She climbed over the pyre and stood with her back pressed against the solid wood of the stake.

The executioner turned slowly and walked toward her pyre. It stopped at the foot of it, holding the torch ready.

"May I see your face, first?" Emma asked.

With one hand, the mystery person pushed back their hood. Revealing...her face.

Emma gasped. "No."

"Your sacrifice is noble," her twin said in her voice. "But it is for naught." The false Emma turned abruptly toward her father's pyre, took three steps and thrust the torch toward the wood. It caught.

"No!" the real Emma shouted. She struggled but found her hands restrained by rope. Where had the rope come from?

The copy of her did not listen. It took several steps toward her mother's pyre and repeated the action.

Emma screamed, trying to fall to her knees but being forbidden by the tight binding of the rope. "Mother! Father!"

"You killed us both," her father condemned her. "All you had to do was choose."

"I thought I was being noble," Emma sobbed.

"You were being a foolish, naive child," her mother scolded loudly over the crackling of the flames.

Her mother's words hit her like a punch to the gut and a slap in the face at once. Her heart raced, her palms began to sweat, and her throat constricted.

I am detecting elevated heart rate. Are you in mortal peril?

The voice would have made her jump had she not been tied up. "Who's there?" she asked aloud. The voice sounded familiar...

Do you require assistance to control the symptoms of your panic attack? The voice asked.

"Panic attack? Who are you and where are you?"

I am Shadow, your Neurological Interface Assistant. Have you received brain damage? I am receiving no optical stimulation through your eyes and can detect no external source for your anguish.

"My parents are burning before my eyes!" Emma shouted to the unknown voice. "Can't you see that?"

One moment, please. Seconds later the voice returned in her head. I have located the source of the intrusion. Attempting to block access now.

The scene before Emma *flickered* and her parents and their pyres disappeared. She blinked and found herself on the ground, facing her twin, who turned to stare at her in shock.

"This is impossible," the voice of not-Emma said. "You must make a choice." The last word came out deeper in tone.

Memories flooded Emma's mind. The forest, the arena, the man-bull, the Sphinx, the golden door. All of it. She fell to her knees and clutched her head as minutes' worth of moments flashed before her at once.

Neural overload detected. Deploying dampeners. The torrent of memories shattered and were just...there, but no longer assailing her. She remembered. All of it. Her parents, her brother, the journey to Tar Ebon, the Tower of the Seven Stars...and the Sorting Chair. "I'm in the Sorting Chair."

I apologize for not detecting the intrusion sooner, m'lady. I have blocked manipulation of your memories, though I cannot physically break the connection yet. This is an advanced simulation device I have yet to encounter.

Do what you can, Emma thought back. I don't think it means to hurt me - it's supposed to test me. If I pass its tests it may release me. "And you're not real." She pointed to the double of herself.

"I am the avatar of the device called the Sorting Chair. You are being tested for selection of your house."

"It feels more like torture," Emma shot back.

"That is why memories are typically suppressed." The avatar cocked its head to one side. "I do not understand how you are conscious of your current state."

"Now that the cat is out of the bag, why don't you release me?"

"I cannot end the simulation until you complete the final stage."

"Is this the final stage?"

"This is the second-to-last stage."

"Fine. End this stage and let's get on with it."

"This stage is not finished. You must choose a sacrifice to test your emotional strength."

Emma gritted her teeth, remembering the face of her father and mother as they burned. *It's not real, though.* She looked the avatar in the eyes. "Bring them out again. Shadow, allow that. I will watch them both burn – will that satisfy you?" She spat on the ground.

The avatar nodded, and the pyres returned, on fire like before. Her parents were bound to the stakes as they were before, only this time screaming.

Emma stared straight ahead, at a point above the avatar's head. *It's not real, it's not real, it's not real,* she repeated over and over. How could any normal person go through this and *not* be traumatized?

The program is designed to wipe the memory of the student being tested after each test. You would not remember the trauma once the stage has ended.

So, it's okay to do this if the person doesn't remember it? That doesn't sound very ethical. She tried to put as much sarcasm into her tone as possible, though she suspected it was lost on Shadow. "You will not break me," she said to the avatar. "I know this is not real."

"I am not here to judge you," the avatar of the Sorting Chair said. "I am here to determine what houses best suit you."

"And don't you have to judge me to do that?"

"I make assessments of your character and capabilities based upon your reactions to stimuli. I do not judge your reactions."

"So, you're making an assessment of me right now, based on how I act to my parents burning in front of my eyes?"

"And your resourcefulness in using another artificial intelligence to circumvent my programming."

He gives me too much credit, there, she thought. She hadn't asked for Shadow and didn't even fully understand what he was. "So what houses will you suggest for me?"

"You have not yet completed your trials. It is premature for me to render my determination at this moment."

Emma rolled her eyes. This avatar reminded her of Shadow. Very by-the-book and rule-oriented. "Fine. Can you speed up the flames?"

"The burn rate is calculated to match that of reality. It was determined by my programmer that a realistic burning scenario would elicit the most visceral, truthful responses from the student."

"Gee, I wish I could meet your programmer," she said, voice dripping with sarcasm. What sort of sick person would create such tests?

"You may indeed meet him one day. My records indicate he is still alive."

"Wonderful."

"Would you like to know his name?"

"No." *Because then I might be tempted to seek him out and kill him.* Anger, visceral rage, bubbled up in her. Whose brilliant idea was it to imprison students in a dream-like state where they were tortured four times and left with no memory of the trauma? The anger washed away any sadness at watching her parents die and she watched dispassionately as the flesh melted from their bones and their charred remains crumbled to the ground.

When the last flame vanished, an indeterminable amount of time later, for time worked differently here, even with her memory restored, the avatar spoke. "The third trial is complete." The pyres disappeared, along with the remains of her parents. A glowing circle appeared on the ground behind her captor. "Please step into the circle to proceed to the fourth trial."

"It's not like I have a choice," Emma grumbled. She brushed past the body that looked like hers and intentionally hit the avatar with her shoulder. Or intended to, for her shoulder passed through the avatar as if it weren't there. *Great. A ghost is my captor.*

It is not a ghost. It is a holographic representation of the Sorting Chair's central processing unit, Shadow replied.

You can go back to being quiet now, Emma replied as she stepped into the center of the ring of light. Just keep me from forgetting all this, will you?

I shall remain vigilant and silent.

The world flashed around Emma and morphed into an indoor location. Stone walls, pillars, a high vaulted ceiling. Orbs of light floated high above her, spinning around one another in a metallic dance. *What is this place?* She wondered, hoping Shadow would not reply.

Not-Emma did not reappear. Emma considered shouting to call the mind of the chair out but was interrupted by frigid wind and streams of black dust flowing past her. The dust materialized into a figure, cloaked and with its hood up. It seemed taller than the avatar had been in Emma's form. "Is that you, avatar?"

"No," her own voice came from the side. She stood dressed in the same clothing Emma did in front of a pillar. "This is the master mage. The fourth trial is one of magic."

"I'm ready," Emma said.

"That is what ninety percent of students say when entering this trial."

"And the other ten percent?"

"Say nothing."

"I wonder which are braver. What is the test?"

The master mage, a dark mage by the looks of his attire, answered her question a moment later when the air around her became noticeably cooler. He then launched a large fireball at her. It shrieked through the air, sounding like a whistle.

Emma focused on what she'd been taught, but the fireball looked so large and came so fast that she had no time to attempt to counter it with her own magic. Instead she was forced to leap aside at the last moment, fearing her clothing would light on fire, and let the ball slam into the wall behind her.

The enemy mage gave her no time to breath in relief. Another fire ball came, but this time split into three as it flew. *That's stupid*, Emma thought. *Only one will have a chance of hitting me*. An instant later the two outlying balls curved inward toward her, as if they knew where she was or were being directed by the mage's will. "Shit." This time she closed her eyes and drew upon the magic that was always there at the back of her mind. She sensed the elements of existence that composed the balls of fire - superheated air blurring faster than her eyes could track. Could that be part of it? What if she could slow the elements within the fireballs down? Would that cool the fire? But she didn't know how to do that. Absorbing the fire, like she'd done to Ethan's fire ring, was not an option. *Not if I want to live, anyway*. Could she die in the simulation? What other choice did she have? She was running out of time, for though time seemed to slow while using her magic, the fire balls still lumbered toward her, being mere feet away.

What if I absorbed the heat? The enemy created the fire by focusing heat from the room into specific points, or in this case, orbs. What if she created something so cold that it absorbed the heat? But how? She'd seen something similar done by Alivia but hadn't see how it was done.

When mother wants to cool iron she thrusts it into buckets of water. That absorbs the heat, raising the temperature of the water. What if...she delved deeper into the elements of existence surrounding her and there she found it - water. Water, if she could draw it to one place, could absorb the fire, couldn't it? She had to try or face burns. Even though she knew it wasn't real, she didn't want to be burned.

Emma raised her arm and cast her awareness far and wide throughout the strange building she found herself in. The drops of water spread through the air like a blanket. She *pulled* with her magic, summoning the drops of water and at first nothing happened. Then one drop pulled closer, and another, and another, and more, and more and more until a torrent of water droplets raced toward the space in front of her hand. She cracked open her eyes and beheld a wall of water floating before her. Just in time, too, for the flames, which seemed to home in on her position, slammed into the wall of water at that moment. Water flash-boiled to steam and the steam swirled back toward her before disappearing, depositing droplets of warm water on her skin.

The mage across from her did not react, either in shock or otherwise. He stomped the ground and it shattered, sending cracks streaking toward her.

Emma leapt out of the way as the cracks sliced through where she'd been, leaving deep gouges in the floor large enough to swallow a person. If that attack hit one of the pillars... *Enough of this*, she thought. Enough of being the victim. It was time to take the fight to her foe. But how? This was a test designed for students, young students, right? So, what would a ten-year-old with limited magical knowledge do in a situation like this? Stand there and "die?" She looked up. A chandelier hung above the enemy. Considering the nature of this dream, that wasn't coincidence. A rope ran from the top of the chandelier to where it was tied, a ring along the wall to Emma's right.

Taking a deep breath, Emma ran behind the first stone column and peaked around it. The enemy, unperturbed, launched a ball of ice toward her. She ducked back and moments later heard a ting like glass shattering as the ball struck the column, chilling it further. She took advantage of that moment to slip around the column and run to the next one, where she waited but heard nothing. She looked around that column and found the enemy holding a ball of lightning above his head. "Shit." She had to move, now! Bursting into action, Emma ran along the right wall, ring anchoring the rope center-most in her mind.

As she ran, a strong tingling sensation washed over her. Her muscles, everything from her arms to her legs, cramped and heat rose from her skin. Looking down, she saw lightning crackling over her skin, connected in a ragged stream to the ball above the master mage's head. She collapsed as the lightning continued to surge through her body.

Shadow. Help. Every thought came with a mighty struggle as her pain wracked her body. Blackness crept in from the edges of her vision.

Dangerous levels of electricity detected. Deploying countermeasures. The surge of lightning, or electricity, as Shadow called it, continued but she no longer felt it. The pain ceased. Was she dying?

You are not dying, Shadow reassured her. I have nullified the effects of the shock on your body while protecting the nerve pathways. You may now walk.

Emma stood, feeling odd not being able to control her legs but seeing them move. It was like rising when sitting on her legs for too long. She knew they were there and could move them clumsily but couldn't feel them completely. She took a step, then another, then another. A glance at her foe showed him continuing his strike. She sought out her clone, the false Emma, and found her waiting by the rope holding the chandelier in place.

"You are deviating from the parameters of the program," not-Emma informed the real Emma.

"Screw you, and your program," Emma said, struggling to speak, despite not feeling the pain from the electricity coursing through her. "I'm...ending this." She reached the rope and untied it. It unraveled, and the chandelier dropped. It slammed into the mage and he crumbled to the ground. The lightning surrounding her ceased, though blackened patches of skin remained.

Commencing repairs, Shadow said.

Feeling returned to her extremities and as she watched the burns on her body faded. *How are you doing that?*

Nanites in your blood are handling the repairs.

What are nanites?

Based upon your limited scientific understanding...

Hey, watch it.

The concise answer is these are small artificial creatures inside your body designed to heal wounds rapidly and keep your body in good condition.

And you control them?

Yes. I am like their brain. Without me they cannot function.

Well, thank goodness for you, then. She met the eyes of the avatar. "I won. Now release me."

"Your ways were...unorthodox," the avatar of the Sorting Chair began, "but you have completed the trials. I shall release your mind and render my recommendation."

"What will the recommendation be?"

"You shall see," the avatar's voice became distant and the room she had occupied disappeared. Darkness met her eyes and she felt something atop her head. She reached up with hands and lifted the helmet off. Her friends and Alivia stood there, anxiously watching her.

"Are you all right?" Kylie asked. "You were shouting, and at one point screaming."

"She can't remember. Remember?" Ethan pointed out.

"I remember," Emma said quietly, drawing a gasp from Alivia. Indeed, the memory of her time in the illusion produced by the Sorting Chair seemed like a dream in the way it tried to fade from her mind. But it was still there, if vaguely, anchored in place perhaps by Shadow.

I can sharpen the memory, if you like, Shadow offered.

You can affect my memory too?

Yes. Much in the way I deflected memory tampering at the hand of the avatar, I can protect and retrieve memories that may be buried in your subconscious or otherwise suppressed.

Well then, go ahead, Emma thought in reply.

The memories returned clearer than they had been before. She remembered every detail. "I remember everything," she amended.

"How?" Alivia questioned.

Emma opened her mouth, intending to share the revelation about Shadow with her, but was interrupted by the same chattering as before that heralded the generation of a verdict by the Sorting Chair. Two pieces of paper fell to the floor.

Alivia picked them up. "The Sorting Chair recommends House Longclaw or House Eustasia."

House Longclaw was the military and weapons and fire house, Emma remembered. "What's House Eustasia?"

"They focus on intellect and the study of chemicals and physical characteristics of our world. Science, as Jason Thorpe put it."

Emma wrinkled her nose. Why had the chair chosen House Eustasia as one of her choices? Just because she outsmarted it with the help of Shadow.

"Who's next?" Alivia asked the group.

Ethan looked at Emma. *What did you see in there?* He asked through the link, making Emma shudder in surprise.

I shouldn't tell you, Emma began.

Come on. I'm your brother.

I'll tell you this. Call on Frank at the first chance you get. It will make things a lot easier for you.

So, you won't tell me what you saw?

Nope. You must experience it to believe it.

He gave the impression of chuckling. *Okay, okay, here I go.* "I'll go next," he said, raising his hand. He approached the chair and sat down. Alivia lowered the helmet, like before, and the testing of her brother began.

A short while later, during which he mumbled unintelligible words, soaked his shirt with sweat and stomped his feet a couple times, the armbands retracted, and he reached up and shoved the helmet. "Okay, that was *not* fun. I'd rather not have remembered the previous tests."

Kylie wore a worried look on her face. "Will I remember?"

"You shouldn't," Alivia reassured her, casting an unreadable glance toward Ethan and Emma.

The Sorting Chair spit out the verdict for Ethan. "House Arreat and House Skycrest."

"Sweet, I choose House Arreat with Richard."

"Don't you want to know what House Skycrest is?" Alivia asked.

"Ummm," Ethan scratched his head. "I guess so."

"The seventh house, it deals with the weather, such as wind, water, lightning and manipulating the storms."

Ethan stroked his chin. "That's actually a pretty sweet-sounding house." He looked to Richard, who shrugged as if to say, "do what you want." Then he shook his head. "Nah, I'll stick with Arreat. Maybe I can be a blacksmith like Mom."

Alivia nodded. "It's settled then. You may pursue House Skycrest next year. Kylie, it's your turn."

Kylie stepped forward and repeated the steps of the other three. She shuddered shortly after the helmet descended, her body shaking fiercely.

"What's happening to her?" Emma asked.

She sensed magic emanating from Alivia and her eyes turned white momentarily. "She is experiencing a trauma of some kind."

"Can you stop the test?"

The arch mage shook her head. "No one here knows how to stop it."

Emma watched, fear welling up inside, as the seizure continued. *I'm helpless*, she thought. *I'm the one who brought her here and now she could die.* She stepped forward, ignoring Alivia's warning, and put her hand on Kylie's. She might not have been able to prevent Kylie from suffering from something, but she could provide some small comfort. She hoped the girl felt it. Kylie's seizures ceased and although her breathing was still heavy she seemed to be faring better than before.

Minutes later, her body went limp and the armbands retracted. She reached up and pushed the helmet up. She blinked, looking at all of them and down at where Emma held her hand. "Did something happen?" she asked.

Emma let out a sigh of relief. Her friend was okay, and with no memory. Just to confirm, "You don't remember what happened during the test?"

The girl shook her head. "No. I sat down and the next thing I know I'm waking up and pushing the helmet off. Did I pass the test?"

The Sorting Chair answered her inquiry by spitting out two sheets of paper like before.

Alivia perused them before looking up. "House Meridia and House Warivia." She held up a hand to forestall questions as to what those houses represented. "House Meridia is dedicated to the study of healing and the human body and diseases that can affect it. House Warivia is dedicated to animals, nature, agriculture and herbalism."

"So, I'm not with any of you," Kylie observed, her face falling.

"You will still have ample opportunity to see your friends. You will share some classes and you will see one another during meals and free time each day. Do not worry."

Kylie's face brightened upon her hearing the reassurance from Alivia. "I choose House Meridia. I've always been fascinated with healing."

Alivia nodded. "Excellent."

Emma did the math in her head. "That is only six houses. What's the other one?"

"House Veritas is the remaining house. It focuses on espionage, diplomacy, law and order."

"So...politicians?" Ethan asked. "The mayor of Ironforge sucked."

"Mages as a rule do not hold political office, and diplomacy does not mean politics. Mages can represent the Federation to foreign nations when necessary and help diffuse tensions."

"Or spy, which is pretty cool. Too bad the chair didn't think I'd be good at that."

"Maybe you're just multi-talented and the chair couldn't choose," Richard said, cracking a smile.

Ethan cocked his head thoughtfully. "You know, that makes sense." He pointed at Richard. "Good thought."

Emma rolled her eyes. Boys. "What's next?" she asked Alivia.

"Now you will be shown to the floors belonging to your house." A dinging reverberated through the courtyard outside the building. "But first it is supper time. Your initiation can wait until after you fill your stomachs."

"Now you're speaking my language," Ethan said, rubbing his stomach. "I could eat a horse."

"Horse doesn't taste good. Too stringy," Richard said.

"It's just a phrase, dude," Ethan replied, using a word their father always used.

"Follow me," Alivia said and led them toward the exit.

Chapter 3

Alivia led Emma and her companions from the outbuilding housing the Sorting Chair. The courtyard was barren now that the returning mages had gone into the tower. She led them across to the ramp leading up to the sliding door Emma had seen before, which slid open at their approach.

"Wow, you even have magic doors?" Ethan asked.

"They're not magic," Alivia replied. "They're remnants from when the Founders built the Tower."

"And they still work?"

Alivia chuckled. "Yes, miraculously they still function. I don't know that anyone except Jason would know how to repair them if they broke."

They passed over the threshold and Emma stopped. She looked up, up, way up, her neck arching back. The center of the Tower was hollow, with a glowing yellow light far above them near the top. Was that the light she'd seen from afar during their approach to Tar Ebon? Around the sides of the tower were balcony-like floors with railings protecting students or staff from falling to their deaths. A grand staircase opposite the sliding doors led to the second level.

The sound struck Emma the most. It was...quiet. Though she saw students moving levels above her she heard their voices like she might hear a whisper. She would have expected a place with a hollow center to be loud because the sound would echo everywhere.

"It's so quiet," Kylie said, sharing Emma's sense of wonderment.

"Acoustic dampeners keep the noise isolated to individual floors. Mostly."

"How many students fall to their deaths every year?" Ethan asked as he looked around.

"Fewer than you might expect. Those railings are not just for show. They emit an energy field which prevents energy and objects, including students, from passing through."

"Nice. The Founders thought of everything, didn't they?"

"They came from a more advanced place than us," Alivia explained. "What little that remained was put to good use here."

"You said something about food," Richard said, surprising Emma by speaking up. He was so quiet!

"Yes. Follow me." She led them around the grand staircase to a set of doors nestled behind them. The doors stood wide open and the room beyond opened into a massive dining hall that, for the second time in a short time, took Emma's breath away.

Seven long tables spanned the length of the room, while another table ran perpendicular at the far end of the room. She guessed that was for the teachers.

"Richard and Ethan, you two are at the first table," Alivia pointed to the table on the far-left side from where they stood. "Emma, you are at the table to the right of theirs. Kylie, you are at the fifth table," she pointed to the right.

Emma gave Kylie a frown and hugged her. "Don't worry, we'll see each other later."

Kylie offered a brave smile and said, "I know," before approaching the fifth table, where she was met by a boy about her age or a little older. Not a teacher?

Emma followed Richard and Ethan and had her question answered moments later when a girl who couldn't have been any older than she approached her.

"Can I help you?" the red-headed girl in a navy-blue uniform with a patch on one side of her chest asked.

"Yes. My name is Emma. I am a new student."

The girl narrowed her eyes. "I didn't hear anything about a new student."

"It was all very...sudden," Emma replied, turning her head to find Alivia. *This girl can talk to Alivia - she'll straighten it out.* She was gone. Frantic, Emma turned and scanned the sea of students and teachers. She found the arch mage striding between two tables heading toward the front table housing the staff.

"And you were assigned to House Longclaw?" The girl had a hint of challenge to her voice this time. Or was it doubt?

Emma turned back to face the girl. She held out her hand. Might as well try to make a good first impression, even if the red-head had no interest in the same thing. "I'm sorry. I didn't catch your name."

"I didn't give it." The girl folded her arms, glaring.

Emma kept her arm outstretched, determined not to be intimidated despite her awkwardness. "May I ask your name?"

The girl rolled her eyes and huffed but finally spoke. "It's Kyra." She still made no move to shake Emma's hand.

Emma nodded and retracted her hand as if the other girl had. "Nice to meet you." *God give me strength to not slap this girl.* "Are you a..." she noticed the patch the girl wore was not present on any of the other students near their end of the table, "an official of some sort?"

"I'm one of the heads of house," she replied. "Formally, we're called prefects. You can refer to us as either. What, did you just get off the boat and walk here or something?"

"So how many heads of houses are there per house?"

"Two. One boy and one girl. Trevor is down at the other end with the first years."

Emma looked to her left and found Ethan and Richard being ushered to the far end of their table. The first-year end. They awkwardly sat down among ten-year-olds. How humiliating. Weren't there exceptions for older students? She tried to see where Kylie had been placed but couldn't find her.

"Professor O'Leary," a voice boomed, belonging to a scrawny man in black robes with gray hair and a crooked nose, cutting through the conversations and bringing silence upon the room. "I see you bring four new pupils. Is that correct?"

Alivia, who now stood before the staff table, amplified her voice also and spoke, "Yes, they come from the east. There was not time to write of their arrival and prepare. But I trust the Tower is up to the task of accommodating them."

"They presume to go to random tables," a female voice said, belonging to a younger blonde professor wearing spectacles but outfitted in the same black robes. "Have they been sorted?"

Alivia nodded. "They have been sorted and have moved to their assigned tables at my direction."

"Yet you did not consult the council before taking such action?" the same woman asked.

"I did not think it necessary, given the circumstances." She paused dramatically. "Will it be necessary?"

"I for one think it is fine, Meredith, Charles," a third voice chimed in. This from a handsome younger professor with black hair. His voice sounded familiar, but the feeling passed moments later. "We cannot turn away willing and able pupils."

"Thank you, Professor Quaith," Alivia said, "for advocating for the ideal this Tower strives to represent. Opportunity for *all* to learn."

The professor she'd called Charles cleared his throat. "Yes, well, although it is unorthodox, we shall allow it."

Kyra spoke, bringing Emma back into the moment. "Well, that settles it then. Welcome to House Longclaw." She gestured to the table. "You'll sit with the first years."

"But I'm sixteen years old," Emma protested.

"And how much magical knowledge do you have?" Kyra challenged.

Enough to sear you where you stand, Emma thought, but suppressed her emotion. "Some. Alivia taught us while we were traveling in her company." And when we were running and fighting for our lives in the wilderness, of course.

"That's Professor O'Leary to you," Kyra corrected her.

Emma blushed, hoping Kyra took it as embarrassment and not anger. She nodded her head. "Of course. Professor O'Leary." She took her leave of the head girl of her house and went where she was directed.

A tall, handsome boy with dark brown hair and blue eyes stood as Emma approached the end of the table. He looked like a giant compared to the younger first-year students among whom he sat. He held out a hand and smiled, showing two rows of straight teeth. "Why, hello there. You must be one of the new students." He looked around her, as if expecting more. "You're the only one assigned to House Longclaw?"

Emma shook his hand. "Yes. My brother and my other two friends are in different houses. I'm Emma. And you're Trevor, right?" She twirled a finger through her hair before realizing it. *What am I doing?* She stilled her hand.

Trevor ran a hand through his hair. "Yep, that's me. Welcome to House Longclaw." He cleared his throat. "Sorry about Kyra. She can be...intense...sometimes."

"That's an understatement," Emma said.

Trevor maintained his smile and gestured to the bench. "There's a spot right here for you." Right next to him.

"Thanks." Heat rose in her cheeks. Shadow, can you stop me from blushing?

I am afraid that is outside the scope of my programming. Unless the blush is caused by poison, infection, disease or another outside cause your nanites cannot affect it. I could suppress your emotions if you like.

No, no, that's okay, she thought. Experiencing emotions was part of what being human was all about, wasn't it?

She took a seat and Trevor sat on her left. To her right sat a young girl, likely ten, as that's the age most first-years were, with silver hair. Emma caught herself staring. She'd never seen silver hair before.

The girl smiled shyly, then touched her hair. "I'm from the Pearl Islands."

"I don't know where that's at," Emma admitted.

"It's midway between the Citadel and Hel'tai."

Emma studied the table. "I'm sorry. I know where the Citadel is," *kind of*, "but where is Hel'tai?"

"Oh, sorry. It's a port on the western coast of Aria, the continent in the far east."

"Oh. So, you're from the middle of the ocean?"

"Yes." The girl smiled excitedly. "I always heard sailors' tails of Tar Ebon but never thought I would see it."

Emma couldn't help but smile in return. "I'm glad I got to see it too." She turned her attention back to Trevor. "How far away do students come from?"

"All over the world," Trevor explained before taking a bite of ham from his plate. "Sagami, the Haguesfort, the Citadel, Tera Leon, even refugees from the Rakosh Empire." He gestured with his head to one girl across from the silver-haired girl with skin pale as snow. "She's from the imperial capital."

"Wow. And I thought I came a long way from Ironforge."

Trevor chuckled. "Nope. Ironforge is close compared to where these kids came from."

Emma's stomach chose that moment to growl. Loudly enough that she feared her half of the table could hear. Certainly Trevor could, she worried.

He smirked. "Let me get you some food." He stood up and walked to a door situated on the wall behind the teacher's table. Spurts of steam emanated from the room, suggesting it was the kitchens. He disappeared inside.

Emma looked around while she waited. Ethan and Richard were already eating, stuffing their faces with legs of chicken or turkey or some other meat. Ethan caught her looking and waved at her. *Boys and their stomachs*, she thought. *How did they get food so fast?* Perhaps their heads of houses weren't such bullies and hadn't delayed them like Kyra did her.

She wanted to stand up to locate Kylie, but feared breaking unspoken rules forbidding such behavior. Instead she looked around at her classmates. Young faces of numerous cultural backgrounds met her gaze. From the tan skin and slanted eyes of the Sagami to the also-tanned skin of the Valnosi to the thick build of the Rovarkian and pale skin of what she guessed was Gallean or Tar Eboni. Would the ten-year-olds be her classmates? Or would she be moved to classes with older students because of her age? Alivia had been scarce on details concerning their academics. Maybe she didn't know herself?

Trevor returned minutes later with a stone plate piled high with ham, a chicken leg and potatoes and carrots. He set the plate down in front of Emma and offered a knife and fork. "Your dinner, m'lady."

Emma's cheeks warmed. "I'm hardly a lady." *I'm not even close to nobility.*

"All fair maidens are ladies in my eyes."

That line caused Emma to almost spit out the first bite of potato she'd taken. She swallowed, then said, "Does that line work on all the girls?"

Trevor shrugged and took his spot next to her on the bench. "Not really. But can't blame a guy for trying."

Emma chuckled. Trevor reminded her of Ethan. She sought her brother out with her eyes and, speak of the Krai'kesh, there he was, standing up next to the House Arreat table reenacting something. She guessed it was their "heroics" during their escape from Senegal Fortress. Or at some other point during their time in the wilderness. She put her hand to her head and covered her eyes. "Ugh, my brother is making a fool of himself."

Trevor pointed. "The guy standing up, waving his hands around?"

"The very same. We, uh, had an adventure during our travels here. I'm sure that's what he's recounting."

"Yeah, he's pointing in your direction. Must be at the part where you did something heroic." His tone suggested curiosity as to what that "something heroic" was.

Emma rolled her eyes. "I'd really rather eat than tell stories. But I promise I'll tell you the story some time."

"I'll hold you to it," he winked and gave his charming smile again.

The two of them were silent for several minutes as she filled her stomach. She took advantage of the silence to listen to other conversations. Everyone spoke at once in the hall, it seemed, so it was difficult to focus on a single conversation, but she heard snippets of the first years talking about this professor or that one and the older students further down talking about going out into the city and buying something called peppermint beer.

A glance up at the teacher's table confirmed Alivia had taken her place there with the professors. She sat chatting with Professor Quaith, the lone vocal supporter of Emma and her friends. She nursed a cup of wine but had no food in front of her. Seated at the center of the teacher's table was an elderly man with a long gray beard and wearing spectacles. He also wore dark purple robes. He watched the students eating, his eyes flickering here and there. They settled on Emma for a moment and he gave her a warm smile. She elbowed Trevor. "Who's the man with the gray beard in the center of the table?"

"That's the headmaster of the school."

"So, he's in charge of the Tower?"

"No. Only the school. The Tower itself is governed by the council of mages. Every teacher, and the headmaster, are part of the council and he chairs the council, but he is not like a king or anything."

"And the queen has no power over the Tower?"

"Nope. There's been a separation of power since the Founding keeping the Tower separate from the ruling family. Not that they haven't tried to control it."

"Oh," Emma said, curious as to what he meant by that. Had they tried to seize the Tower in the past?

"Two of the queen's children are here as students. Princess Feodora is our age and she's in House Veritas. Her younger brother, Prince Hadrian, just started this year. He's in House Skycrest."

"Does the queen only have two children?"

"Nope. She has six, but they're the only two with magic. Her oldest, the Crown Prince Neal, has no magic but turned eighteen recently. Then between Feodora and Hadrian is Princess Salena. She's fourteen. The youngest two are twins, Tristan and Teagan. They're eight, so it's unknown if they'll have magic yet or not."

"You really know the royal lineage," Emma observed.

"It's not a secret. But," he blushed, "it helps that my father is a duke."

"Oh." Idiot, that's all you can say is "oh?" Say something more useful than that.

Are you speaking to me, m'lady? Shadow chimed in.

Did you speak out loud? She asked sarcastically.

No, I did not.

Then I'm not talking to you. She growled in her mind, hoping it translated as fiercely as she thought. She cleared her throat. "I mean, that's wonderful."

"I guess." He studied the table.

"So, it's *not* wonderful being the son of a duke?" Emma pressed. She hadn't said enough earlier. Was she going too far now?

"I mean, it's nice but...I don't know. There's a lot of expectations on me. 'Meet this girl, Trevor. You'll be betrothed to that girl, Trevor. You have to learn your numbers, Trevor.' I sometimes wish I wasn't royalty."

Emma raised an eyebrow. "Your parents are forcing you to marry the girl of their choosing?" She knew that happened. It happened in Ironforge and across the civilized world, as she understood it. Her mother had more than once gone on a rant about women's rights and how backward the "civilized" world was.

"I'm the eldest, so they want to make sure the girl is of good enough blood to marry into the family and become the future duchess of our house."

It made a sort of twisted sense in Emma's mind, but still left her with a pit in her stomach at the thought of being forced to marry someone she may or may not love. "Is your father a duke here in Tar Ebon?"

"No. In Valnaria. He trades in fine wines from his vineyards."

"Is the woman you're betrothed to a mage?"

Trevor snorted. "That's the worst part. She's not."

Emma pursed her lips. That sounded an awful lot like Bloodcloak talk, speaking poorly about those without magic.

The change in facial expression was not missed by Trevor. He held up a hand. "I know what it sounds like. I'm not prejudice, really, I'm not. But it's just that she can't understand what it's like to have magic. It'll be a rift between us, forever, you know?"

Emma nodded. She hadn't thought of that before, hadn't thought of marriage yet, but it did make sense wanting to be married to someone who shared your ability. But, like her father always said, opposites attracted. So, which was the right answer? Maybe there was no right answer.

She opened her mouth to speak but was interrupted by a gong sounding.

"Dinner is over," Trevor said.

"What now, then?" she asked.

"Back to House Longclaw for study and to prepare for bed." He extricated himself from the bench and stretched as the rest of the hall erupted into action.

"I don't even know what classes I'll have tomorrow. Do you know?"

He shook his head. "No, that's not up to heads of houses. The house adviser will decide that. The adviser for House Longclaw is Professor Quaith."

Emma let out a sigh. Good, the nice professor was their adviser. "So, I can talk to him when we get up to our house?"

"Yep. Come on." He led her to where the students lined up, preparing to exit the dining hall.

She stood for a second, eyes flicking to where the students her age stood in line and back to where the first-year students were.

Trevor, guessing her dilemma, led her closer to the front of the line. He placed her in line between a raven-haired girl and dark-skinned boy. He then walked to the rear of the line.

Kyra, situated at the front of the line, gave her a glare before spinning.

The students from House Arreat exited. Ethan gave Emma an enthusiastic wave as they passed, while Emma imparted a more subdued wave to him.

Once their house had left, Kyra walked toward the exit. House Longclaw exited and made their way to the grand staircase.

I wonder how far up House Longclaw's quarters are. She had never been up high before, except for their time in Senegal Fortress. The Tower eclipsed that place ten-fold.

Up the grand staircase they went to the second floor. There they were led to the left and to a corner of the second-floor landing. A staircase was nestled there, slanting up toward the next floor. Up they went to the third floor, then the fourth. They continued going up for, by Emma's count, seven floors. They stopped at the seventh landing and without fanfare the girls and boys separated. The girls continued straight, toward the near side of the eighth floor; while the boys, ushered by Trevor, turned left and made their way toward the far side of their floor. Naturally, Emma followed the girls. A glance over the railing showed students filing into their chambers on the floors below her also.

The girls entered through a single set of doors and Emma gasped. A vast chamber lay before her, with lavish purple carpet covering the stone floor, wall hangings adding decoration and furniture scattered throughout the room. A large window encompassed the far wall. A hallway ran off to the left and right.

Emma stood in the center of the room as the girls separated and went down either the left or right hallway or sat down on furniture. The younger girls seemed to go to the left, while the girls around Emma's age went to the right. She made to go right but Kyra interrupted her.

"New girl. You have to wait to speak to Professor Quaith." She stood by the entrance to the girls' chambers, arms folded.

"When will he be here?"

Kyra shrugged. "He'll be here when he gets here."

Great, thanks for the precise answer there, Emma thought. "What is your problem with me?"

Kyra blinked, then frowned. "I noticed you talking to Trevor. Stay away from him."

Is she deflecting? I hadn't even talked to Trevor when she met me and acted like she hated me. "I wasn't interested in Trevor." Okay, that's a lie. "But you were against me the second you saw me. Why?"

The prefect of House Longclaw pointed a finger at Emma. "You come in, years after students start, and expect everyone to just accept you? You're not going to fit in. You should just go back to the hole you crawled out of."

"And what made you think I liked Trevor?" A suspicion took hold in her mind. "Do *you* like him?"

"He's too good for you."

Deflecting again.

"Yeah, he's the son of a duke. So what? If I wanted to court him I could."

"You wouldn't be a servant in his father's estate, let alone his wife."

"Oh? And what's your pedigree?" Emma's face burned as though it had been exposed to the sun all day and she was half-tempted to have Shadow suppress her emotions to avoid from punching Kyra in the face.

She puffed up her chest. "I am the daughter of a count."

What's with royalty and mages?

"The count of what?" *Bitches and snobs?*

"The count of House Valcrest."

"Am I supposed to know where that's at?"

Kyra huffed. "The Crossroads. He's in charge of the operations for one of the merchant houses."

Emma brought up a mental map and located the Crossroads, southwest of Tar Ebon at the southern edge of the western woods across the river. From what her father told her, it was a crossroad between the four cities of Shar'Hai in Sagami, Mara Damare almost straight south of the Crossroads, Valnos at the mouth of the Tar River and Tar Ebon. It was a major hub for trade. "Are you betrothed to Trevor? He said he was betrothed."

"Not yet." Kyra smirked. "And you're not going to mess it up for me, either."

So what, you're going to steal him away from his betrothed? And I don't like him. She stepped toward the girl, ready to give an angry retort, when the door opened.

The dark-haired Professor Quaith stood there. He wore a set of tan robes with the hood down. He smiled at Emma. "Oh, hello. You must be the new student, Emma, yes?" His eyes seemed to twinkle.

As before, his voice sounded familiar, as if she'd heard it before. But she pushed the thought aside. She'd never met the man before. Instead she focused on his white teeth and smiled in return. "Yes, that's me."

Professor Quaith clapped his hands in excitement. "Excellent! Welcome to House Longclaw." He dropped his voice to a loud whisper. "The most powerful house in the Tower."

"Why? Because of the military and fire magic focus?"

"But of course. None can match us in the art of making war."

"Some would argue peace is the better option most of the time." Her mother's face flashed in her mind.

"Yes," the word came out in a hiss, "but war always comes. History shows us this. Every civilization has gone to war at some point in their history. And," he held up a finger, "they've either survived or perished."

Kyra nodded off to the side.

Emma pursed her lips. She disagreed, but now was not the time to argue with the adviser of her house. Instead she forced a smile and nodded. "You make a good point." *Time to change the subject.* "Since I'm new here, and so much older than the first-year students," *a fact Kyra delights in rubbing in my face,* "what classes will I be taking?"

He had begun nodding halfway through her question but waited to speak until she was done. "Yes, Alivia spoke to the other advisers and I about the matter. I advocated letting you jump in at the level representing your age group. Some of the others," his mouth curled, "did not like the idea of that and recommended you start with beginner classes."

A lump formed in Emma's throat. It's not that she didn't want to be in class with the first-years, but she would feel out of place there. "What was the verdict?"

"A test. To evaluate your magical potential. Alivia spoke highly of the magical prowess of you and your friends in the wilderness, just a few days past, and so we will test your knowledge in the essential areas to assess where you should be placed."

Emma sighed. *Thank God.* "Great. When do we start?"

Professor Quaith laughed. "So eager to begin. Get some rest tonight, then we will test you tomorrow."

Emma nodded. "Of course." One step closer to my dream becoming a reality.

Chapter 4

After Professor Quaith left, Kyra reluctantly showed Emma to her quarters. Well, her bunk, as she shared quarters with three other girls. Fortunately, the girls were her age. There was Joceline, a short blond-haired Valnarian girl, Agnes, a tall, scrawny Gallean girl with tattoos on her face and Kaveri, a hulking Rovarkian.

"Welcome to House Longclaw," Agnes said, offering a crooked smile. Joceline ignored her. Kaveri grunted and offered a nod in acknowledgment.

"Thank you," Emma said, smiling in return and trying to ignore the sting of being ignored and barely acknowledged by the other two. Kyra left without a word and Emma undid the belt at her waist containing what meager possessions she owned and placed it on the bottom bunk of the bed assigned to her. Agnes, it turned out, slept in the top bunk.

"So where are you from?" Agnes asked, maintaining her smile.

"I'm from Ironforge."

Joceline snorted. "A backwater in the middle of nowhere."

Emma felt her cheeks warm at the insult but resisted the urge to provide a sharp reply. Just because Joceline was likely from Stoneridge or Valnos, much larger cities, that didn't give her the right to make fun of Emma. "Yes," she agreed. "Full of small, close-minded people." *So much for not giving a snarky reply.*

Joceline sniffed, actually sniffed, before exiting the room.

"Don't mind her," Kaveri said grumbled in a deep bass voice. "She is a snob."

"Thanks. I got that," Emma said.

The thick girl grunted.

"Do you know what classes you're taking?" Agnes asked, seemingly unperturbed by Joceline's comments.

"I'll find out tomorrow." She did not elaborate. "I need some air. Excuse me." She made for the door.

"There's a common area for all the houses on the ninth floor," Agnes offered.

"Thanks." Emma left and walked down the hall to the sitting area of House Longclaw. She exited and went to the stairs, though she noticed a set of shining doors with no handles on the wall between the girls and boys areas. *I wonder what that is.* A pair of buttons glowed in the wall next to the door. She continued into the stairs and walked to the ninth floor.

The common area consisted of an open room wherein the central shaft of the Tower was dwarfed in size. Instead of walls or hallways the entire width of the tower was open. Tables and chairs and couches sat in clusters throughout, while bookshelves lined the wall opposite her. To her left and right the far walls were pure glass, giving a dim view of the outside world as the sun set. Dozens of students occupied the chairs and couches. She might be able to get some air here, but not necessarily any privacy.

No one paid her any mind as she went to an open armchair and sat. She observed how the students interacted, with boys and girls generally remaining separate and students of similar age grouping up.

Ethan? She reached out through Shadow.

Yeah, what's up, Emma? Ethan asked a moment later.

Are you awake?

Obviously.

Are you okay? Settled into House Arreat?

Oh yeah. They're really cool here. Richard and I have some interesting roommates.

I'm glad your experience has been better than mine.

Her brother fell silent for several seconds. *What's wrong?*

Emma blinked away tears. It's just not what I expected, that's all. Did you hear they're testing us for placement tomorrow?

Yeah, but I'm not worried. Are you? Is that what you're upset about?

How could her brother be so unobservant? No. It's just...some of the girls aren't the nicest.

Eh, just ignore them.

Easier said than done.

Well...listen...word on the street is there's a steam ship in town. One of the new ironclads. First time one has ever been to Tar Ebon. Richard and I were going to go down with Cadmon and check it out.

Our first night here and you're already causing trouble?

Oh, come on, Emma. We're not getting into trouble. We're just going to sneak aboard and grab an up-close-and-personal look.

A look at what?

The steam engine. How it works. Aren't you curious?

She really wasn't. But...I guess. Anything is better than just sitting here twiddling my thumbs.

Awesome. Where are you?

Up at the common area on floor nine.

Oh, there's a common area?

Yeah, it's nice. Lots of students here.

Okay, well, how about you meet us on the ground floor and we'll go?

How are we going to avoid detection?

We're not prisoners here, Emma. We can come and go as we please. That's what Cadmon says. As long as we're back before curfew. Still a few hours left. Come on.

Emma sighed, physically and through the link. *Fine. I'll meet you there in a few minutes.*

Awesome. The link closed, and Emma was again left with her own thoughts. Should she try to find Kylie? She hoped her friend didn't feel abandoned by her. She hadn't had a choice in what house the Sorting Chair chose for her. None of them had. *She's in House Meridia.* If House Arreat was on the eighth floor, and House Longclaw on the seventh, that suggested House Meridia was located on the fourth floor of the Tower. She again went to the stairs and walked as quickly as she could to the fourth floor. Arriving there, she guessed the girls' dormitory would be on the same side as it was on her level. She knocked on the door. It opened and a dark-skinned girl with braided hair stood there, brown eyes looking her up and down.

"Can I help you?" the girl asked.

Emma cleared her throat. "Yes. I'm looking for Kylie. She's new and..."

"One minute," the girl interrupted her, shutting the door in her face.

Rude.

Several minutes passed before the door creaked open, revealing Kylie in a nightgown. Where had she gotten that? She smiled at seeing Emma. "Hey."

"Hi," Emma said, not knowing what else to say in the moment.

"Are you settling in?" Kylie asked.

Emma shrugged. "A little. Some of my roommates are not very nice, though."

"Oh."

"Where did you get that nightgown?"

"One of the girls gave it to me. She knew I didn't have anything."

"That's nice of her." I doubt anyone but Agnes or Trevor would even give me a drink of water if I were parched and in the middle of the deserts of Sagami.

"Did you need something?"

"Yeah." Focus, Emma.

Would you like an infusion of chemicals to help focus your brain on the task at hand? Shadow interrupted. I have a host of options to stimulate your brain.

Not now, Shadow. "We, I mean me, Ethan and Richard and a guy they met, Cadmon," she was babbling, "are going down to the harbor to try to catch a glimpse of the iron clad that just steamed in. I know it's kind of boring, boy stuff and all, but...well I'm already feeling a little stuffy in here, you know? Do you want to come?"

Kylie smiled. "Sure, I'll come." She looked down at her attire. "Just let me change, okay?"

"I'll wait out here."

Kylie disappeared back inside the dormitory for House Meridia, shutting the door behind her.

Emma tapped her foot as she waited, then walked over to the railing and looked over it, or tried to, but an invisible barrier blocked her. *Oh, right, safety barriers.* Instead she looked up, toward the floors higher up. She saw the occasional student walking past the railing on the upper floors.

The door opened, and Kylie stepped out, dressed in the same traveling clothes she'd worn when they arrived. When would they be getting new clothing? "Ready."

Together they walked down to the first floor and found Ethan, Richard and a third boy, who must have been Cadmon, waiting there for them. Cadmon wore a turban covering his head and possessed dark skin. She guessed he was from Sagami, probably in the south, near Aran'Pier where people who looked like him tended to come from. She made a note to thank her father for owning numerous books talking about the cultures of the continent of Tar Ebon when she was a girl, though she did wish she'd learned more about the wider world. The boy bowed upon seeing them, then reached for Emma's hand. She jerked it back. "What are you doing?"

"Kissing your hand," he said, perplexed.

"Ummm...no thanks."

"Forgive me," he bowed.

"Don't be rude, Emma," Ethan chastised her, smirking. "Let the guy kiss your hand."

Did he kiss your hand? She thought to herself. "Fine." She extended her hand and he planted a quick kiss on it, then looked to Kylie expectantly. She reluctantly extended her hand and he repeated the gesture. *I guess it's supposed to be chivalrous?* "So what, we just walk out?"

"Yes," Cadmon said. "The curfew is not for three more hours. So long as we have returned before then we are safe."

"Great. Let's hope we don't get lost."

"Trust Cadmon," Ethan said. "He knows his way around. Right, buddy?"

Cadmon inclined his head. "I am quite familiar with the city, yes."

"Lead the way."

The boy led them out the main doors and west, toward the declining sun. The warm air wrapped around her. She hadn't realized how cool the interior of the Tower was. They exited through the western gates of the courtyard and found themselves on a straight street curving downward. The harbor lay in the distance, visible due to their height advantage. It disappeared as they continued walking. Aside from the inns and taverns they passed, most of the shops had begun closing, with villagers returning to their homes, or going to the local inn or tavern for a drink, for the evening.

"This is Harbor Street," Cadmon commented as they walked.

"Aptly named," Emma observed. "Since it leads to the harbor."

"How did you hear about the steam ship?" Ethan asked.

"I have many contacts in town. I come from a long line of merchants. "

Does everyone come from royalty or merchants around here? Emma wondered. Does nobody come from ordinary peasants? "When did you discover you had magic?"

"When I was ten, like everyone." He eyed her, and she got the feeling he was staring primarily at her chest. "Well, like most people. My parents put me on a ship and sent me here. My uncle was already here running merchant operations for my father, so they got me off the ship and took me to the Tower. The rest is, as you say, history."

"Nice." *Must be nice. We lose six years of training and start late, while everyone else is so far ahead of us.* It didn't seem fair. Why couldn't her magic have manifested at age ten like the others? Would her parents have been able to afford to send her to the Tower, though? Or would she have ended up in a coven like the one Kylie came from? And what would have happened to Ethan? That begged the question, how many children or teenagers like her were out there having developed magic but never been trained? Were there other secret covens or groups of mages in the world other than the Tower? Factions of mages? She'd seen firsthand how the Cult of Rae utilized dark mages to carry out their bidding. Were they evil or were they misguided children turned evil by the wrong upbringing? "Nature versus nurture," her mother would call it, before pointing out that the matter was seldom cut-and-dry.

"Are you doing okay?" Emma asked Kylie as they walked.

They passed a tavern emanating raucous sounds. *That's probably where the sailors go at night*, Emma thought.

Kylie shrugged. "It's only the first day here, but yes, so far I'm enjoying my stay."

"I wish I could say the same. The head girl of my house is a wench. She doesn't like me at all and claims I'm going after Trevor, the prefect of our house."

"Oh. I'm sorry to hear that. Are your roommates nice?"

"One is nice. Another ignores me and the third is super quiet."

"We don't have that problem," Ethan chimed in. "Do we, Richard?"

"No. Everyone is nice in our house."

Emma rolled her eyes. "How nice for you." It didn't invalidate her own experiences, however.

"It is," Ethan agreed.

"She was being sarcastic," Richard said.

"At least someone is paying attention," Emma said.

Ethan's reply was forestalled by Cadmon speaking. "We are here."

Indeed, they stood at the entrance to Tar Ebon harbor. Dozens of ships sat moored there in the dim light of dusk, many with gangplanks lowered. Emma had seen smaller ships that plied the Iron River, but never big ships like what floated in the harbor. Cadmon pointed out their target near the northernmost pier. It did not appear to be guarded.

As they neared, Emma found herself admiring the steamship. Its shape was like that of the other ships in the harbor, but there the similarities ended. The hull of the ship, instead of wood, appeared to be made of iron. Metal smoke stacks emerged from the center of the ship, blowing a thin trail of gray smoke into the air. She would not want to breathe that in.

They walked down the pier and Cadmon went right up the gangplank. Kylie hung back. "I don't think this is such a good idea," she said.

"Oh come on, what's the worst that can happen?"

"We could get caught," Emma said, siding with her friend. "They could imprison us."

"Then why did you girls agree to come along?"

To get away from that infernal tower and those girls, Emma thought. Instead she said, "We wanted some fresh air, that's all."

"Fine. Stay here, chickens." They started following Cadmon.

Emma shared a glance with Kylie. "I mean we did come all this way. Aren't you at least a little curious?"

Kylie sighed. "Fine, let's go in."

The two followed the boys and found themselves on the wooden deck of the steamship moments later. *So, it's not made of metal, just plated with metal.* An eerie silence hung over the ship, with a thin plume of smoke emerging from the smokestack being the only source of movement. "Where is everyone?" Emma asked.

"At the tavern or asleep," Cadmon said. "That's why we chose now to come."

Emma couldn't shake an ominous feeling that had settled in her gut. "You're not afraid of getting caught?"

"We're just taking a peak. Come on." He led them toward a stairwell and they crept below deck. The halls were deserted, lit by infrequent lanterns in glass enclosures. With fire being such a threat aboard a ship, even one with metal plating, it was understandable to limit the amount of flames that could be tipped over and start a fire.

They had gone down two floors when they reached the bottom and found a door rimmed with light. That had to be the source of the steam. Indeed, Cadmon led them toward it and put a hand on the latch. "Get ready," he whispered.

Emma tensed, expecting someone to be in the room. Surely they would have someone tending the fire that produced the steam, wouldn't they?

Alas, the door opened silently, revealing a metal construct with fire glowing behind a large iron door. No one occupied the room. Emma let out a sigh of relief.

"Look at that," Cadmon said, voice dripping with excitement. "They call it a 'boiler' because it boils water to produce steam that turns something called a 'turbine' which in turn causes a propeller to spin and make the ship move faster than it could under the power of wind."

"So exciting," Emma said, yawning. Maybe she'd have been better off staying at the Tower. *I could be in bed right now.* She glanced at Kylie, who looked just as bored.

The boys were not bored, however. Ethan rushed up to the boiler as if greeting a cute girl, then proceeded to open the door, releasing a rush of sweltering heat into the room. Richard was not far behind, coming to stand beside his friend and talk shop. They pointed at pipes running up from the deck below and more stretching from the boiler section into the ceiling. *Like kids in a candy store*, she thought.

"Who are you, and what are you doing on my ship?" a female voice came from behind.

Emma spun and gasped. A girl her age stood there barefoot with a cloak wrapped around her and her black hair cut above her shoulder. She glared at them with green eyes and held a pair of daggers in her hands.

"Well, what are you doing here?"

The boys, having heard the newcomer's voice, stumbled over to the doorway and peered out. "Shit, we've been caught," Ethan said.

Thank you Mr. Obvious, Emma thought. "Who are you?"

"Don't try to deflect," the girl said, waving one of the daggers around. "I'm the one asking the questions here."

"My name is Emma," she touched her chest. "These are my friends, Kylie, Richard, Cadmon and my brother Ethan," she indicated each with a finger.

"What are you doing aboard my ship?"

"Your ship?" Ethan asked. "You're awfully young to own a ship."

"And you're awfully young to be trespassing on a ship. Didn't your parents teach you any manners?"

"We were just curious," Emma explained. "We aren't here to cause any harm."

"You wouldn't have gotten as far as you did if you were," an older, more mature voice said. A woman appeared from the shadows a moment later and lowered her hood.

Emma gasped. "Bridgette?"

The shadow walker smirked. "Forgive my daughter. She tends to have a temper."

"Mom!" the girl exclaimed. "They're intruders. Why are you apologizing for me?"

"Because they're about to be your classmates, Isabelle."

"What?" Her mouth hung open. "You mean *they* are mages."

"In training," Emma chimed in.

"Yes," Bridgette confirmed. "They're students of the Tower. I allowed them to get as far as they did because I know them from earlier this week."

"Wait. They were at the battle you and Dad went to?"

"He wasn't," she waved a hand dismissively at Cadmon, "but these four were quite central in the defeat of the Cult of Rae."

"The battle you wouldn't let me go to," Isabelle said, deadpan. "But they're the same age as I am." Her voice took on a tinge of whining.

"I didn't bring them there," Bridgette replied dryly. "I was there to rescue them. So don't try to twist this around, dearest daughter."

"Ugh," Isabelle groaned.

"We should be going," Emma said. Then she remembered what Bridgette had said about classmates. "Is it true? That she's going to be at the Tower?"

"Yes. She starts tomorrow. We were going to bring her today, but we steamed into port late and I wanted her to get a good night's sleep before tomorrow. I see that plan went awry."

"Well, if you need anyone to show you around..." Emma began.

"I won't," Isabelle replied sharply.

"...I'd be happy to help you," Emma finished.

Isabelle sniffed.

"She can be stubborn sometimes," Bridgette explained.

"Which I get from you," Isabelle said.

"Your father is awfully stubborn. Perhaps you get a double dose from the two of us."

"Dad, stubborn? He's a pushover."

"Have you ever tried to get him to eat when he's working on a new invention? It's like trying to make a mule move faster."

"Whatever." Isabelle rolled her eyes.

Bridgette looked back at their intruders. "Did you have any questions before you go? About the engine."

The boys shook their heads in unison, too intimidated to speak.

"Good. Because I probably wouldn't be able to answer them very well, and Jason is busy working on the next improvement for that engine and might be grumpy right now. Now run along and, next time, don't sneak aboard a ship without permission. It's not polite and is likely to get you hurt."

Emma and her companions walked past Isabelle and her mother and back up top. The ship still lacked activity. As they walked down the gangplank Ethan spoke, "so *that* is Bridgette's daughter? Wow, she's cute."

"Did you *see* the pair of daggers she was holding?" Emma asked.

"A dangerous woman is an attractive woman," Cadmon said.

"Oh? I didn't see you so chatty with Bridgette back there. In fact, it looked like you were going to piss your pants."

"There is such a thing as too dangerous," he hedged.

Emma shook her head. *Boys.*

They made their way up Harbor Street in the dark. Emma couldn't tell what time it was or how close to missing curfew they were, but she guessed it had to be close. The gates to the square around the Tower were still open though, which was promising, and they were not challenged by anyone as they re-entered their home-away-from-home.

Emma made for the stairs.

"Wait. You don't want to take the elevator?" Cadmon asked.

"The what?" Emma asked.

"Elevator. It will get you to your floor much faster than the stairs." He pointed to a pair of silver doors with a seam between them and two glowing orange circles next to them on the wall. The setup was identical to what she'd seen on her floor and Kylie's floor. He stepped up and tapped the top button. It glowed a brighter orange and a sound like something sliding or falling came from behind the silver doors. Moments later the doors separated at the seam, revealing a small rectangular room inside. Cadmon beckoned them inside.

Emma gingerly stepped inside the elevator and stared up. A glow emanated from the ceiling, while a series of buttons with numbers sat to the right of the open doors. The doors slid shut after the five companions had entered, giving Emma the feeling of being shut up in a closet. Cadmon hit the number four and the elevator jolted, and Emma's stomach sank, and her feet felt as though they were being pressed into the floor. A ding emanated from above the doors and she saw more numbers there. One through...fifty. Fifty floors to the Tower? Or were there floors not accessed by the elevator?

The elevator stopped at the fourth floor. "Here's your floor, Kylie," Cadmon said.

Kylie nodded and gave Emma a smile. "See you soon."

"Sleep well," Emma told her friend. She watched her walk toward the door to House Meridia until the silver doors closed, obscuring her view.

Cadmon hit the number seven, causing it to light up orange. Again the elevator ascended and after three dings the door opened to the floor housing House Longclaw.

"Thank you for the ride up," she said, then paused. "Do you know what's further up? Like at floor fifty?"

"The quarters of the staff and their families," Cadmon said, stepping in the path of the silver doors to prevent them from closing. "I think. Classrooms go up to floor twelve, the training arenas are on floor thirteen. Students aren't permitted above floor thirteen unless invited by a professor."

"Oh." She slipped past Cadmon and waved at them. "Thanks for the adventure, boys. We'll have to do it again sometime."

Cadmon winked at her. "You betcha, princess."

Emma laughed. "Hah, I'm hardly a princess."

"You'll always be a princess in my eyes."

Emma felt her cheeks burning as the elevator doors slid shut. She wandered back to the doors to House Longclaw. Sure, Cadmon was cute, but he wasn't really her type, was he? Did she even *have* a type? "I don't know," she answered herself aloud.

She went right to her quarters and found it already darkened. Her roommates were asleep, with Kaveri snoring. She laid down and exhaustion hit her like a wave. Tomorrow would be trials for placement, which she didn't expect to be easy. She welcomed unconsciousness when it came minutes later.

Chapter 5

Emma awoke the next morning in the clothing from the day before. One day in the Tower and already she'd gotten in trouble. Granted, no one from the Tower knew of her late-night escapades; still, it didn't set a good precedent, did it? She would need to find some new clothes soon.

The other three girls were still sleeping when Emma padded out of their quarters and into the common area. Only two girls were there, both poring over the same book and furiously jotting down notes. Were they studying diligently or cramming at the last minute? What good were notes when training to be a mage? She wandered over, intending to peek at what they were doing. The papers in front of them had numbers written on them. Many numbers. And dashes and slashes and other symbols Emma didn't recognize. "What is that?" she asked.

The first girl looked up at her in surprise, a tinge of annoyance on her face. "Math homework, what does it look like?"

The other girl hushed her. "That's the new girl," she said in a loud whisper.

"Oh. Sorry." She didn't sound sorry.

Emma knew her numbers, but what they had written there seemed more complex than addition and subtraction, multiplication and division. "Sorry, I'm just not used to seeing math that complex."

"It's advanced mathematics. Called algebra."

"Ah." *Do you know algebra, Shadow?*

Of course. Would you like me to upload an algebra module?

You can do that?

Yes. It will accelerate your learning of the subject immensely.

58

Emma was sorely tempted. Being able to learn algebra, or perhaps other topics, quickly would be nice. But...*No, thank you. Not right now. I'm here to learn and I'm going to try to learn on my own first.*

Of course. The offer is available at any time in the future.

"Do you know where I can get some new clothes?"

The girls, who had turned back to the book between them, both looked up and assessed her clothing. "You can ask Kyra."

"Thanks." *Great. The girl who hates my guts. She's more likely to give me rags to wear than usable clothing.* She would have to find new clothes on her own. Maybe Trevor could help. She left the girls' quarters, followed the railing around the central shaft and found herself in front of the boys' quarters. She knocked, then realized that there might not be anyone awake within.

Her fears were proved unfounded a few moments later when the door opened and Trevor stood there in a blue night robe. "Emma? What's wrong? Are you okay?"

Emma's cheeks burned. Did he think she was a damsel in distress? She shook her head. "Nothing. I mean, yes, I'm okay, nothing is wrong."

"Then why are you here?" he asked, perplexed. "Girls aren't allowed in the boys' dormitories, and vice versa." His body blocked the way into the dormitory.

"I know that," Emma said hastily. Perhaps too hastily. *Gosh, he's going to think I'm here for...that.* "I just had a question for you."

"Oh." He visibly relaxed. "What's your question?"

His reaction stung her. *Does he not like girls? Or just not like* me? "Clothing. Kyra doesn't really care for me, and I could use a new outfit. Do you know where I can find new clothes? The girls in my dormitory said head girls or head boys could requisition clothing."

"Yeah." He scratched at the scraggly fuzz on his chin. "On the first floor, to the right when you get to the bottom of the stairs, is the laundry room. That's where the fresh clothing is. Here, let me write a requisition request for you." Without waiting for her assent, he disappeared inside, letting the door click shut behind him. He returned a minute later with a hand-written note. He offered it to her. "Here you go. And for what it's worth, I don't think Kyra hates you."

Then you don't know much about girls. She hefted the note. "Thanks for this."

He smiled. "Any time." He closed the door gently behind him.

Emma walked toward the stairs. She didn't hate the elevator but didn't feel comfortable using it alone. Besides, the exercise would do her good. She considered stopping at the fourth floor to check on Kylie but decided against it. They would see each other at breakfast. She reached the ground floor and, ignoring the wonderful smells wafting from the main dining hall, she turned toward the laundry room and entered through a wooden door. Inside, women in light blue uniforms hurried between massive wooden buckets filled with water, soap and clothing and large metal boxes emitting a hum. Clothes spun around inside one of the boxes, visible through the circular window in the front. "What is that?" she blurted.

One of the women, with an arm full of wet clothing, stopped and followed Emma's gaze. "That's a dryer, honey."

"A dryer? What does it do?"

"It dries the clothes," the gray-haired woman said kindly.

"You've been here six years and you don't know how we launder your clothes?" a younger woman with crooked teeth asked.

"I'm new," Emma said defensively. Do I need to wear a sign around my neck announcing that I'm new to everyone I meet?

I cannot help you with that, Shadow interjected.

I wasn't asking you, Emma snapped. But then she chuckled. Here she was arguing silently with the voice in her head. He was the only person in the Tower who wanted to help her.

"Ummm...I came here to ask for new clothes." She offered the writ from Trevor.

The older woman threw the load of clothes in her arms into an open dryer and took the note from Emma. She brought the note up to her eyes and squinted. "New clothes, eh?" She brought the note down and studied Emma's current attire. "Yes, those clothes won't be laundered. They'll be incinerated."

Emma's cheeks burned with embarrassment. She didn't think her clothing had been *that* atrocious. "Oh," she squeaked out.

The kindly woman went to a pile of folded clothes and lifted a tunic. She unfolded it and held it up, as if measuring Emma from a distance. She set that tunic back and picked up another one. That one apparently satisfied her, for she draped it over her arm and went to the trousers.

One thing that had surprised Emma was that here girls and boys alike wore trousers and tunics. In most other places girls were expected to wear dresses. Emma herself had been a bit of a tom boy, and her father encouraged her to wear what she felt comfortable in. There were robes for both boys and girls to wear, but it seemed like those were for formal occasions and not daily life.

After lifting three pairs of trousers, the older woman brought the pair she'd selected to Emma and offered them. "Here you are, deary. Try them on."

Emma looked around. "Here?"

"No, in the dining hall," she said sarcastically. "Of course here. We're all women here, you've nothing to fear from us humble servants."

Emma eyed the other wash women before undressing and taking the clothes she'd been offered. She dressed quickly and watched as her old clothing was carried to a hearth at the back of the room and thrown in. *Symbolic of my coming here. Burn the old to make room for the new.* She nodded to the woman. "Thank you for your help."

"Of course, deary. You tell old Margery any time you need help, ya hear?"

Emma smiled and left the room. Even after such a short time there was a steady flow of students tromping down the stairs. The elevator dinged and a gaggle of students, who must have been crammed inside on the ride down, emerged. She followed the flow of students into the dining hall and first looked for Kylie. She didn't see her, so sought out her brother and Richard. She found them seated at their table. Much like the day before, Ethan waved his arms around wildly and molded them into the shape of a ship. Emma groaned. *Can he keep anything secret?* If he went blabbing about their blundered infiltration of an ironclad from the night before and a professor overheard they could be in deep trouble. Did they suspend students here? Would they kick a student out for going too far? She hoped she never found out.

She made her way over to the table seating the students from House Arreat and stormed up to Ethan. She grabbed his arm and pulled him near the wall.

"One second, guys," Ethan said. "Cadmon can fill in the rest." He gave them a thumbs up before turning his attention to Emma. "What's up, sis?"

"Why are you blabbering about the ship? Did you tell the whole school we snuck aboard?" She looked over his shoulder toward the scarcely occupied table where the professors were seated.

"Relax. We didn't tell anyone we snuck aboard."

"Then what did you tell them?"

"Well. Ummm...that they invited us aboard for a tour."

"You *lied*."

"It would have been a lie to stay silent," he pointed out. "They asked me what I did last night."

"A lie of omission! A white lie! Instead you go and build an even bigger lie! What's next? Are you going to tell them you're the tour guide for the iron ship?"

He stroked his chin. "That's not a bad idea. With our money stolen..."

Emma punched him in the shoulder. "Don't even think about it."

"Okay, okay. I'll go tell them the truth."

"No," Emma said hastily. "You'll just make it worse. Just keep your mouth shut, okay? Unless you want to get suspended."

Ethan pressed his lips together, signifying that he would keep his mouth shut.

Emma sighed. "Go on, get out of..." a commotion among the students, during which they turned and looked toward the door to the dining hall, caught her attention. She followed their collective gaze.

"Isabelle," Ethan said.

Emma half-expected him to start drooling. "Remember what her mother said - she's not your type."

"I'll be the judge of that," he said as if in a trance.

Emma rolled her eyes, which she found she did a lot, and watched as Alivia led Isabelle toward the administration table. Even the professors had stopped eating and watched the procession of two. *How does everyone else know who she is? I guess the black clothing is a little odd.* Maybe word of the iron ship in the harbor and who was aboard had spread faster than she thought. Or perhaps Isabelle's enrollment in the Tower had been announced previously? Emma wasn't sure but was eager to speak to the assassin's daughter to find out. If she would speak to her. They hadn't exactly gotten along aboard the ship, had they?

Alivia turned when they reached the head table and Isabelle stood dutifully in front of her, head held high and staring straight ahead. Emma couldn't read her emotions. Did she *want* to be there or not? "This is Isabelle Thorpe. As many of you know, she is the daughter of two famous Eternals and heroes of the Federation. Please join me in welcoming her to her new home."

Applause erupted from the students, with some of the boys even whooping. Alivia waited several seconds before making hushing motions and speaking again. "The Sorting Chair has recommended House Longclaw and House Veritas. She has chosen House Longclaw."

The students of House Longclaw clapped. Kyra wasn't there, but Trevor had freshly arrived and clapped as hard as the students he oversaw. Professor Quaith approached from the door and ushered Isabelle toward her assigned table.

"Be good," Emma said to Ethan and, not waiting for a response, she returned to her table. She sat down as Isabelle arrived. She caught the newcomer's eye and offered what she hoped was a reassuring smile.

For her part, Isabelle smiled but her eyes were focused on something over Emma's shoulder. When Emma looked behind her she saw that Trevor was the object of Isabelle's gaze, and the target of her smile, not Emma. *Of course. Go for the same cute guy me and Kyra like. Kyra won't be happy about that.* Part of her wanted to be jealous of the girl and treat her like she had treated her on the ship the night before. But another part of her, the part that remembered her mother's words of wisdom over the years, resisted that notion. "Treat others like you would want to be treated," had been one of her mother's phrases, a phrase which she practiced most of the time, even when facing down armorers from the forges who would infrequently visit her at her smithy. While they were yelling at her, with Emma listening in secret from the other room, her mother would patiently listen and respond to their complaints. Yes, she had lost her temper a couple times, but no one was perfect.

Isabelle sat further down the bench from Emma, prompting her to scoot over by her. "Hello," Emma said.

Isabelle glanced at her and raised an eyebrow. "You again."

Emma smiled nervously. "Yep, it's me."

"Here to cause more trouble? Are you even allowed to be in here?"

Emma forced a laugh. "Yes, I'm allowed to be here. And no, I'm not causing any trouble." *Not right now, anyway.* "I did want to offer my help if you need it. I know I've only been here a day more than you, but I've learned some things, like where to get fresh..."

"Thanks," Isabelle cut her off. "But I think I can manage on my own."

"Well, yeah, I'm sure you can, but..."

"You can go now." The girl glared at her.

Emma's head snapped back as if she'd been slapped. "I'm just trying to be nice."

"I don't need nice people."

"Fine," Emma growled, rising from the bench and going to get food. She considered getting Isabelle some, just so she could spit in it, but decided against it. *Be the bigger girl.*

The dining hall started to fill up, with more students filing in. The noise level went up accordingly and soon a dull roar made eavesdropping on conversations a table over impossible. Emma focused on eating and tried to block out the noise. They had their placement test today. She hadn't asked Ethan if he was nervous. Would Isabelle face a similar test today? Or would hers be tomorrow? She looked over at the girl, who had gotten her own plate of food and was currently stabbing at a slice of ham with a belt knife.

Instead of enraging herself further, Emma sought out her brother. He sat among his friends, like before, Cadmon to the right, Richard to the left. They'd moved on to a different story now, one with, was that a bow? No, a crossbow. Ugh, the story of their first encounter with the Bloodcloaks, by the sound of it. *Those boys are worse gossips than girls.*

Trevor sat next to Isabelle and she was actually speaking to him. The rest of House Longclaw gave Emma space and talked among themselves. *It'll just take time for them to adjust to me being here*, Emma thought. Even as she thought that, Kyra entered and stalked toward Isabelle. *Finally, someone else to draw Kyra's ire instead of me.* It had only been a day, but she was already sick of the glares from the girl.

Kyra came to stand directly behind Isabelle and tapped her foot. Neither Trevor or Isabelle seemed to notice. This only enraged Kyra further, though, and she tapped her foot impatiently. Still no reaction.

She cleared her throat, loudly enough that Emma, several students down, could hear it. At last Trevor jerked in surprise and turned. Isabelle turned more leisurely, as if she'd known the head girl had been there all along. Had she been baiting her?

"Who are you and what are you doing with Trevor?" Kyra asked.

Trevor rose and faced her. "Kyra. This is Isabelle. She's in our hou..."

Kyra held up a hand to cut him off before he finished. "Let her explain."

Isabelle didn't rise. She stayed where she was and rolled her eyes, causing Emma to grin. *Yeah, stand up to her.* "I'm the new student."

"*You're* the daughter of the assassin?"

They must have spread the word of her arrival before we showed up. Or gossip spread like lightning when she got here.

"You got it." She turned back to face her plate and stabbed a sausage with her knife.

"Don't turn your back on me. I'm the head girl of your house."

"The head nanny, you mean. You're not the boss of me."

Kyra clenched her jaw and pulled Isabelle's hair, yanking hard.

Oh shit, Emma thought, rising from the bench.

In an instant Isabelle had the knife at Kyra's throat. Her hair was still in Kyra's hand. "Unhand me unless you want to lose your hand."

"Bring it, wench." She a hand out to the side and a ball of flame formed there.

Emma, without thought, summoned her own ball of fire. *Touch her and you burn,* she thought.

Trevor tried to shove the girls apart. "Okay, okay, break it up. Let go of her hair, Kyra. And Isabelle, put away that knife!"

Both girls resisted his efforts to physically separate them and continued glaring daggers at each other.

Emma stepped close. "Hurt her with that fire and I'll hurt you in return."

"Enough!" Professor Quaith's voice boomed, surprisingly deep given his more easy-going smile and normal tone. The difference was enough to shock the girls, and Emma, out of their blood lust. Emma's fire extinguished and Kyra's disappeared a few seconds later.

The man stormed around the table and down the aisle. A glance toward the head table showed Alivia standing along with some of the other professors. She shook her head in what Emma could only imagine was disappointment. "What are you three doing?" Professor Quaith demanded when he reached them.

"She started it," Isabelle and Kyra said in unison.

"I just came to support Isabelle," Emma explained.

Isabelle shot her a glance. It held surprise. Was she surprised Emma had come to support her and not Kyra? *Trust me, I hate her as much as you clearly do*, she thought. If they made it out of this without being expelled she would explain that to her.

"She didn't respect me, Professor," Kyra protested.

"So you did what? Prepared to burn her? What have I taught you?"

Kyra turned her eyes downward. "'Emotions are for the weak. I must master my emotions to master my magic.'"

Professor Quaith nodded. "Good. You reacted hastily, *emotionally*, but you recognize your error.

Is he her personal tutor? Or is he like this with all his older students?

"Now you two," the professor pointed first to Isabelle and then to Emma. "Your first and second day here respectively and you're already turning to violence as a solution to your problems. I am disappointed, to say the least."

Emma hung her head in shame. He's right, but she started it. But that shouldn't matter, should it?

"She started it," Isabelle said, vocalizing what Emma had been thinking. "She wants to start with violence, I'll finish it."

"There are better ways to resolve conflict than with weapons. You must learn to control your emotions and view all the options. Sometimes the hardest, but best, decision is to hold your tongue, or your hand, and wait."

"I won't let her trample all over me," Isabelle said defiantly.

"Did you hear nothing I just said, child? It is best for you to remain silent while I am lecturing you."

For once, Isabelle remained silent, though she continued to lock eyes with the professor.

"Do you wish to talk back also?" he asked Emma.

Emma, who had been watching the exchange unfold with her head down, shook said head. "No. I'm sorry for my behavior."

"A wise answer." He paused for several seconds, and then looked across the dining hall. "What are you all looking at?" he asked in a booming voice. "Get back to eating."

Around the hall, students found interest in their breakfast plates, though the cacophony of before did not return.

Satisfied that his orders were being carried out and the perpetrators were disciplined, Professor Quaith nodded, turned briskly and walked back to the head table. Most of the other professors sat down, with only Alivia continuing to stand.

Emma returned to her seat, while Kyra went back to the head of the House Longclaw table. Isabelle sat back down but Trevor went to the far end of the table, like a dog with its tail between its legs. The remainder of breakfast passed without incident and the noise level in the dining hall slowly rose to where it had been previously before the skirmish.

A gong sounded. Emma looked up. "What was that?" she asked aloud.

One of the students, a twelve or thirteen-year-old by the looks of her, spoke to her for the first time that morning. "It's the call for breakfast to be over and to get to our first classes."

"Oh." *So, does that mean my evaluation is about to begin?* She waited as the rest of the students cleared out and the kitchen staff came out to ferry away the dirty dishes. In the end, only Ethan, Richard, Emma, Isabelle and distant Kylie remained of the students. Three professors stood with Alivia in front of the head table and Alivia gestured for them to approach.

"As some of you may be wondering, today is your placement trial. It will determine which grade level you will be at and therefore which curriculum you will pursue while at the Tower."

"So, if we fail this we could end up with the ten-year-olds?" Ethan asked.

"There are some basic classes you will have to take regardless but based upon your assessed skill level you may be able to test out of some of the classes."

"Niiice," Ethan said.

"Do we do it all at once?" Isabelle asked.

"No, the test will be for each of you separately. Now come, follow me."

Chapter 6

Alivia led Emma and her companions out of the dining hall. The other three professors, the advisers of the relevant houses, followed.

"Are you okay?" Emma asked Kylie, eying the professors behind them, who maintained a distance of several feet.

Her friend nodded, but bags under her eyes suggested the opposite. "It was just a rough night."

"Why?"

"I kept hearing something, a noise, coming from behind the walls. No one else heard it or believed me. Did you hear anything?"

"No. I was too tired. I passed out and slept through the night."

"Lucky you."

"Is everyone still being nice to you?"

Kylie shrugged. "The head girl of my house is nice, but the head boy is like a military drill sergeant. Luckily I don't have to interact with him."

"I wish I had it that way in my house. Instead the head girl hates me."

"Yeah, you told me, and I saw the fight."

"That was a pretty sweet fight," Ethan whispered back toward the two girls. Meanwhile Isabelle, the one who had technically started the fight, walked in front of the boys.

The two hushed as they reached the elevator, which on the ground floor was next to the entrance to the dining hall and crowded into it. It rose to the thirteenth floor and, with a ding, the doors slid open.

The students were led out and to a door opposite the elevator doors. Inside, they found a vast chamber sporadically filled with metal columns evenly spaced. The chamber extended from window to window on the right and left and a wall of windows sat on the far wall. The room seemed to extend around the corner on both right and left. Did it curve around to cover the entire floor?

A gap in the center of six pillars seemed larger than the others. That was where Alivia led them. She faced them. "This is the Ring of Judgment." She pulled a lever built into a pillar and a wall of faint light grew out of troughs in the floor and surrounded the group. It was bright enough to be seen but transparent enough so that all the pillars and other details outside the Ring could be seen.

"Each student will face off against the adviser for their house within the Ring. They will test both your academic knowledge and your physical knowledge. I will make notes and keep track of your performance." She passed through the Ring of light and pulled the lever, extinguishing the light. "It is not a physical barrier but is symbolic of the testing area." Then she gestured for them all to join her outside the perimeter of the Ring.

"You didn't give us any time to study," Emma said.

"There are no right or wrong answers here. This is a test of your baseline knowledge and you will not be penalized for wrong answers."

Other than being put in classes with the young students, she thought. But she nodded, as she didn't want to make a scene.

"Who would like to volunteer to go first?"

"I will," Kylie said, stepping forward.

"Professor Spurling?"

The gray-haired professor who had spoken out against Emma and her friends when they first arrived stepped forward. He scowled. "Of course *I* would be the first to test them." He pointed a gnarled finger at Kylie. "Don't expect me to go easy on you."

"Of course not, sir," Kylie said deferentially. They both crossed over the trough surrounding the Ring and Alivia pulled the lever. The barrier of light sprang into existence.

Professor Spurling harrumphed before speaking. "What do you get when you combine eye of newt with sage tree oil?"

"I don't know," Kylie admitted.

"Professor..." Alivia warned.

"What? I wanted to see how willing the girl was to admit her ignorance. Grudgingly, she passed."

"I don't understand," Kylie said, admitting her ignorance for the second time in a row.

"It was a trick question," the professor explained briskly. "We do not use such crude components in our chemistry studies."

"Oh." She shuffled her feet nervously.

"The actual question is this: when you combine baking soda and vinegar what happens?"

Kylie pursed her lips.

They expand, Emma thought. When they were younger their father had shown them a clay "volcano" filled with the stuff. She remembered clapping excitedly. But Kylie wouldn't know that, would she? Baking soda and vinegar were difficult to obtain items that her father had ordered specially from Tar Ebon - she remembered because she'd seen the receipt and heard her mother chastising him for the indulgence.

"Well?" the professor prompted.

Emma resisted the urge to open her arms wide, like an exaggerated yawn, to give her a hint.

Kylie shook her head at last. "I don't know."

The professor nodded, and Alivia made a mark in the notebook she held.

"Are you going to tell her the answer?" Emma asked.

"No. That is what my class is for, Dear." He held up a finger to cut off any protests. "Next question. What are the components of steel?"

Were these questions meant for me, not her? It's carbon and iron. But again, though Kylie had grown up underground, she was unlikely to know the components of steel.

"Iron and...copper?"

"Incorrect." Another look toward Alivia followed by more scribbles in the ledger.

Try giving her something related to her house, you old prick.

"Now something any aspirant of House Meridia should know by your age. What causes the bloody cough?"

That was a question Emma did not have an answer to. She'd heard of it. Seen it first-hand. Her father called it tuberculosis but hadn't said what caused it. Tuberculosis wasn't the answer, though. It was what caused it.

"Exposure to others with the sickness?" Again, she sounded like she was guessing.

"Partly correct. Half point. And now," his eyes turned white and he summoned a ball of fire to his hands. "Catch this." He lofted it toward her. It sizzled as it flew. It was the size of a baseball her father and Ethan used to throw. Emma had shown no interested in the "sport" of baseball and resisted her mother's suggestion she include herself in the ball throwing.

Kylie took a step back, in panic perhaps? Then her eyes turned white and she lifted her left hand. The ball of fire homed in on her hand and stopped before striking flesh. It floated there, spinning around, the flames licking at an invisible barrier holding its energy inside. She brought her eyes up to meet the professor's.

The professor nodded in approval, his eyes turning back to normal. "Good. Full point. Now extinguish it properly."

The girl, eyes still white, brought her right hand to hover above the flame, sandwiching it between her two hands. Then she slowly lifted her right hand while lowering her left hand. The flames stretched to fill the ever-widening gap between her hands until it appeared to be a sheet of flame. Then she flung her arms wide and the flame sheet winked out of existence. A wave of heat passed through the barrier and washed over Emma and the others. She had transferred it into the air.

"Well done. You know your magic. Fire magic, and a single attack, anyway. Let's try something a little more complicated." Without further explanation he summoned a ball of ice in one hand and a ball of flame in the other, the same size as before. He cast them out and they arced to the side and then moved in a lazy arc toward Kylie.

Kylie, whose eyes had not returned to normal, did not move her head as if watching each ball. She could sense their position in space relative to her. She cast out her arms, perhaps intending to do what she'd done the first time.

But the professor was ready for that move. He made his hands look like claws and brought them close to each other. Lightning sparked between his fingertips before forming into a flashing, strobing ball of harnessed lightning. He cast *this* ball out and it traveled faster than the eye could see, or Kylie could react. It struck Kylie in the chest just as her elbows bent and she flew backward, through the barrier of light, and skidded to a halt when her back hit the wall.

Emma gasped and ran to her friend. "Kylie, are you all right?" She extended her hand to help her friend up.

Kylie, eyes returned to normal and, looking dazed, remained where she was. "Wha...?" she asked, then her head slumped to the side and her eyes closed.

"What did you do to her?" Emma asked, rounding on the professor.

He looked beyond her to Kylie, concern absent in his eyes. "I taught her, and by proxy the lot of you, an important lesson. Always be vigilant. She thought she sensed all I was throwing at her and was surprised by my lightning strike. In battle the strike would have been stronger, and she would be dead right now. She is merely stunned."

Emma looked to Alivia now. "You sanction this treatment of your students?"

Alivia's eyes, normally so kind, took on the look of steel as her eyebrows furrowed. "What I sanction is not your concern, Emma. Please remember your place here."

"She could have died!" Emma shouted.

"The professor would not have allowed that to happen. I was monitoring the energy levels he was using the entire time. He never once strayed outside safe bounds."

"But..."

Alivia held up her hand. "Leave it alone, Emma. Remember your place here."

Emma's cheeks burned, and she imagined she looked as red as a tomato. She looked to her friends, but Ethan shrugged helplessly and Richard shuffled his feet and studied the stone floor. Isabelle returned her gaze but chose that moment to roll her eyes. *Cowards and the heartless daughter of an assassin. Wonderful companions you have, Emma,* she thought. She gritted her teeth and turned back. "Yes, ma'am." She offered a mock bow.

"Are there any further tests for Kylie, Professor?" Alivia prompted.

"No."

"Then kindly take her back to House Meridia and allow her to rest and recover."

The professor bowed, walked to Kylie and laid hands on her shoulders. Emma suspected he was lending her strength or healing her of the damage she sustained from his attack. *Making up for what you did to her, eh?* Kylie regained consciousness and rose. Then, limping and leaning on the professor, she exited the exam room.

"Who is next?" Alivia asked, smiling.

You mean who is the next victim? Emma thought sarcastically.

"I'll go," Ethan said. He sauntered forward without waiting for an invitation and entered the Ring. His eyes focused on Professor Wimble, the blond-haired woman who was adviser to House Arreat. "Bring it on, Professor."

The younger professor snorted as she strode into the Ring. "Such confidence will be your undoing, young student."

"You going to ask me some questions first?"

Professor Wimble smirked. "I prefer questions under pressure. Her eyes turned white and she cast her hands out and downward. The ground trembled and the chamber shook. "What are the ingredients for steel?"

That question again? Well, I guess Kylie hadn't answered it.

"Easy. Carbon and iron. My mom was a blacksmith."

"What is the melting point of iron?"

"Uh..."

Twelve hundred and four degrees, Emma urged mentally. Mother would remind Father how hot it was in her forge when he complained that he was hot slaving over the stove all day.

"...three thousand degrees?"

"Too high. Did the quake distract you?"

Ethan scratched his head. "I'm not sure I knew it to begin with."

"Next question." The dust which had fallen to the floor rose like a cloud and shot toward Ethan. "How do you make a metal stronger with magic?"

Ethan shielded his face as a hailstorm of accelerated dust and chips of rock slammed into his body. "Owww!"

Another cloud rose and swarmed toward him. "Well?"

"I can't think!" he shouted, then spit out dust as it filled his mouth. "You hammer it more!"

"Wrong again." A small vortex of stone and dirt formed, with the dirt and dust from around the room streaming toward it. "Now disassemble this vortex unless you want to know what it feels like to suffer dozens of tiny cuts."

Ethan groaned. "I didn't sign up for this!"

The vortex advanced, twisting and swaying back and forth as it neared her brother.

Finally, his eyes turned white and he thrust out his hands. The vortex stopped moving toward him, through it still spun. "There, I stopped it!"

"You must disassemble it."

Use your own wind to match its rotation with a counter-rotation, Emma thought. That should slow it enough that the dirt will fall to the floor. She was sorely tempted to open a link to her brother and reveal that to him. But that would be cheating. What did that make them if they cheated during the placement trials? It wouldn't help them in the long run. So she kept the link closed and watched.

Ethan tried hurling fire at the vortex, but that resulted in a flaming vortex. "Shit. Think, Ethan, think," he muttered to himself. He looked toward Emma. "What would you do?"

Emma shook her head, reinforcing the decision she'd made. "You have to do this on your own."

Alivia nodded, apparently approving of Emma's restraint.

I still don't forgive you for Kylie, she thought, not smiling.

"The clock is ticking," Professor Wimble said. This time two more vortexes appeared and moved toward Ethan, one from each side. This seemed to surprise him enough that his concentration was broken, because the initial vortex, now on fire, continued its path toward him.

As the three vortexes converged on him he screamed.

Emma took a step forward and seized her magic. But what she sensed stopped her from taking any further action.

A bubble formed around Ethan. He was not screaming in pain, but instead screaming in anger as a wall of air rebuffed the three vortexes. The shield drained the energy from the attacking spells, as seen by flashes of light Emma could sense, and soon the vortexes, and the flames, had faded. He released the shield and Emma released her hold on her magic.

"Well done," Professor Wimble smiled. "A uniquely defensive solution to the problem at hand. I am impressed." She looked to Alivia. "I have no further trials for the boy."

Alivia nodded. "So be it. Ethan, you may return to House Arreat. We will deliver your class schedule to you later today or tomorrow."

Ethan gave a mock salute. "Got it, your eminence." Then he winked as he passed by Emma and the others and on to the elevator.

"Emma? Will you go next?" Alivia asked.

Emma swallowed and nodded. She entered the Ring of Trials. Professor Quaith followed and faced her.

The dark-haired professor who had advocated for her and her friends when they first arrived at the Tower would now test her. Instead of questions like Professor Spurling or an attack mingled with a question like Professor Wimble, he began with a test of magical skill. "Show me how well you can create a shield," he ordered. He then summoned lightning like Professor Wimble had.

Emma called upon her magic and felt it there, sparking between his fingertips. She imagined a shield, an energy field that would block the lightning from hitting her. She didn't know quite how she did it, only that she was confident it would block the coming attack.

Indeed, the lightning arced toward her a moment later and slammed against her shield, crackling and covering its entire surface. "Good," Professor Quaith said. "Now harness the lightning and send it back to me."

That request almost caused Emma to release the shield. Harness the lightning? She had only had experience dispelling attacks with magic, not turning it back on her attacker. She supposed it must be possible, but she never had. Not wanting to fail, she thought hard, trying to think up the answer. She sensed the elements of the lightning there, crackling beyond her shield, but they felt foreign to her. Like they didn't *belong* to her. That was silly though, wasn't it? The elements composing her shield didn't belong to her, not really. So what defined ownership of an element of existence? Maybe willpower? She willed herself to seize control of the lightning. Nothing happened. She tried to wrap her senses around the lightning. She could feel it, could feel the elements, fading now that the connection to the magic from Professor Quaith had ceased. She didn't have much time before the lightning would fade completely.

She embraced the lightning with her mind and directed her magic toward it. The lightning renewed its crackling journey across her shield with new fervor and it now felt as if she "owned" it. But how to re-direct it? Right now, her magic was feeding it, but she could sense heat emanating from it as it faded into the air. She had to do something with it soon or it would drain her energy. *What if I try to wrap the lightning inside the shield? Like an orb to contain the energy?* She warped the protecting shield, curving it so that it became a self-enclosed orb with the lightning continuing to crackle within. Then she sent the entire orb containing the lightning toward Professor Quaith.

While she could not see the professor's expression, she suspected he was surprised. He stopped the shield encasing the lightning in mid-air and did *something* to dissolve it. Then he clapped, bringing her back out of her magic-manipulation trance. "Well done. Now a question of history. Who won the Battle of Nymidia in 30 AF?"

Emma closed her eyes and wracked her brain. Nymidia, in present-day Sagami, over a thousand years before. She'd read of it only in passing and her father had never specifically taught her anything about it. *I know it had something to do with the Founders versus another group, but that's not specific enough. Every battle is about one group versus another group.* She sighed, hating to say it, "I don't know."

The professor nodded. "No shame in that. What divides the northern hemisphere of our world from the south?"

"The storm wall," she replied without hesitation. That was easy. Her father had shown her maps as a child of the "known world," with a barrier symbolized at the bottom of the map labeled "storm wall."

It was said to be a near-impenetrable wall of storms. Legends told of sailors who had made it through and returned to tell the tale, but they were often left mad, babbling nonsense about the dead walking and other unbelievable tales.

"Good." He withdrew a dagger and tossed it to the ground. It slid toward Emma and stopped a few feet away. "I want you to freeze the blade."

"Not melt it?" Emma blurted.

"No. The opposite."

She picked up the dagger and studied the metal. It looked like an ordinary iron dagger. She drew upon her magic and studied it further with her senses. Indeed, she could see the space between the elements of iron that made up the dagger. The elements vibrated slightly, as though they were shaking in unison. Was that due to heat? Like a heat haze that always surrounded her mother's forges? If she stopped the vibration of the material, would that reduce the heat? She tried to focus on stopping the elements of the iron, but it felt like trying to grasp a tuning fork, but one that would not stop shaking. She let go, her head hurting from the vibration. What if she cooled the air around it? Would it leech the heat out of the metal? She tried, but as she cooled the air around it by removing heat she noticed no noticeable change in the vibration of the iron. She was about to try again when the professor interrupted her.

"That is enough for this trial. You did not pass, but you will one day learn the proper way to do it."

I didn't know there was a time aspect, she thought. Or was I so far off the mark he wanted to spare me further embarrassment? She didn't know for sure.

"You may exit the ring," Alivia said. She continued to jot down notes.

Well, two out of four isn't bad, right?

"Richard, you're up next."

Chapter 7

The remainder of the trials had passed without incident. Richard had done poorer than the others, getting only one question right and failing the magical tests. Isabelle, on the other hand, had aced the questions and the magical tests, leaving Professor Quaith looking impressed. Emma had suppressed a tinge of jealousy watching her succeed so handily.

She tested out of geography 101, defensive magic 101 and defensive magic 102. However, that still left her with a long list of classes to juggle. Seven classes in all for this year, and she was starting several weeks late.

Now Emma sat in one of her first classes, World History, learning in excruciatingly boring detail all about something called the "Valnos Rebellion," in which the Valnarians living there sought to annex themselves from the country. Of course, the Valnosi nobility had not allowed that and had sent an army to crush the rebellion. Hundreds of civilians were killed.

"Lies!" a boy at the back of the class shouted. He was a dark-skinned boy who looked to be ten or eleven years old. "My people have never sought to leave Valnaria."

"History is written by the victors," Professor Ratwatte pointed out. Their professor was a short olive-skinned woman with her black hair worn in braids. Emma could not place her ethnicity. "Here at the Tower, we record the history of all conflicts and events in a fair and balanced manner. We do not embellish or twist the facts."

"Your story is fake," the boy insisted. "I am saying it never happened."

"My dear child," the professor began, far more patiently than Emma felt she would have given the circumstances, "this conflict occurred hundreds of years ago. It is not a representation of your people now."

The outspoken boy took a moment think over what the professor had just told him. "How do you know it actually happened?" he pressed.

"We have books, my dear, with eye-witness accounts of the events. We have copies of the ledgers of war from both sides. We have letters soldiers wrote to their friends or family and dispatches between the Valnarian capital and their field armies."

"All of that could be falsified," the boy argued.

Emma rolled her eyes, wishing she could rise up, walk over to the boy and slap him silly.

The professor, clearly seeing Emma's reaction to the boy's argument, held up a finger. "Now, now, students, do not mock this boys argument. Wrong as he may be," she held her finger up higher, to forestall the boys protest that he wasn't wrong, "he deserves dignity in our response to him."

I could bow to him before I slap him, she thought.

"If I stab him in a dignified way, will that work?" Isabelle asked from two rows behind Emma and to the right. She sat in the same row as the arguing boy. When Emma looked back, the assassin's daughter was glaring daggers at the dark-skinned boy.

The professor did not dignify Isabelle's question with a response. Instead she focused on the boy and spoke. "Based upon the number of verifiable sources gathered from numerous locations we must conclude that the events actually happened. Did we see it with our own eyes? No, for as I said it was hundreds of years ago, but if we do not place our trust in verifiable documentation of historical events we must question everything. It would require us to question whether the Founding really happened, whether the storm wall exists, whether the Krai'kesh exist even. All of that would come into question for those born after the battle with the Krai'kesh if we could not trust written accounts of those events. Do you understand?"

The boy did not respond. He maintained eye contact with the teacher, his cheeks turning red, before he at last turned his eyes down toward the desk and did not respond other than with inaudible mutters.

Did the idiot finally see reason or is he just picking his battles? The muttering suggested he would regurgitate his opinion about fake history another day, probably when least expected.

"All right. Now then, let's move on to the..."

"MAKE SURE TO ALWAYS wear your safety goggles, vests and gloves. Magical shields can fail if you lose consciousness and have other limitations. Physical protection is therefore required." Gray-haired Professor Spurling eyed his students warily, as if expecting them to strip down any second and attempt chemistry naked.

Emma looked to her table-mate, Kylie, while donning her gloves. "Are you ready to make something together?"

Kylie shrugged. "I guess."

Emma frowned. Her friend had seemed saddened for the past several days. Ever since their placement trials. *I don't think I've seen her smile in four days*, she thought. "What's wrong?" she whispered.

Kylie spoke as she put her vest over her head and pulled it down. "I failed so many of the tests."

"Oh. I failed some too, so don't feel bad."

"That doesn't make me feel any better. Yes, I know *some* magic, but I had trained with the coven for years. Was my life wasted there? I know so little about the outside world and even mundane things like what makes up other things."

"That's not mundane. We're learning stuff here that I guarantee most farmers in Tar Ebon know nothing about. Well, maybe farmers know about steel, but not about chemistry or medicine." She smiled reassuringly. "Don't beat yourself up."

The former coven witch smiled. "Thanks, Emma."

"Today we are mixing a substance called ammonium nitrate and water." The professor held up a brown paper packet. "This is the ammonium nitrate. Its creation is an advanced chemistry magic technique that requires extracting its constituent elements from the air and other sources. If you work hard in this class and pass you may begin progress to advanced chemistry where the elements of these chemicals are studied and manipulated. But for today, you will combine this prepared compound with water to demonstrate a method of absorbing heat. The resulting cold can in turn be manipulated by you as mages." He placed a packet on each table before continuing. "On each table is a glass beaker. That is where you will add the ammonium nitrate, followed by the water. You *must* wear your safety equipment before doing this. Begin by opening the pouch containing the granules."

Emma unrolled the top of the paper pouch and peered inside. White granules inhabited the dark interior.

"Pour the compound into the beaker."

Emma complied.

"Now, carefully and slowly pour the water into the beaker."

Kylie lifted a beaker containing some water and poured it into the first beaker. At once, the beaker began to boil.

"Now touch the beaker. How does it feel? Touch it with the back of your hand!" he snapped at one student who had whole-heartedly gripped their beaker.

Emma gingerly put the back of her hand near the beaker. Immediately she felt cold. "Cold," she said aloud. Others echoed her observation.

"Yes! The reaction of the ammonium nitrate and water creates what is known as an endothermic reaction. Meaning it absorbs heat from around it. This is not magic, but the resulting absorption of heat can allow *you* to more easily summon ice or frost magic or can act as an absorber of fire magic."

"So, we can direct a fireball to a beaker and it will absorb the heat from the fireball?"

"Yes..." the professor said slowly in answer to Emma's question. "But, you do not want to be too close to the reaction point. When ammonium nitrate is heated enough it turns into a gas that will impair your thinking for a time. But if you have enough ammonium nitrate that it does not reach the boiling point of water when met with a fireball, you will have succeeded in countering the spell. Now, let us continue..."

"CAN ANYONE DEFINE AN obtuse triangle for me?" blonde-haired Professor Wimble asked her class.

Emma looked around at her classmates, who in turn were looking around themselves. Ethan, seated across the aisle from her, shrugged.

One of the girls raised her hand.

"Yes, Clemence?"

"An obtuse triangle is a triangle with one obtuse angle."

"And can you define an obtuse angle?"

"An obtuse angle is an angle that is greater than 90 degrees," the plump red-haired girl answered dutifully.

"Teacher's pet," Ethan grumbled under his breath. Emma couldn't help but giggle.

"Is something funny?" Professor Wimble asked, eying first Emma and then Ethan. She was the adviser to House Arreat, her brother's house, and had witnessed Ethan's sense of humor first-hand.

Ethan straightened up and coughed, looking like he was trying to appear innocent. "No, Professor. Nothing is funny."

Emma merely shook her head.

The professor sniffed but continued. "Excellent answer, Clemence. Extra credit points for being the *only* one to know the answer." She clasped her hands behind her back. "Some of you are new, so you have an excuse," her eyes fell on Ethan and switched to Emma, "but for others, some of whom have repeated this course," her eyes fell on a table next to them occupied by Kaveri, Emma's hulking Rovarkian roommate, and another girl she didn't recognize, "this should be review." She suspected the professor was speaking to Kaveri in particular, a suspicion that was confirmed a moment later when the broad-shouldered girl shrugged and grinned.

Mathematics was her most boring class yet. History had its place when learning about the world and why it was and possibly where it was going. Chemistry could create compounds that could be used to assist in the casting of magic. But mathematics. When was she really going to need to know what an obtuse triangle was while casting magic? Perhaps if she was designing buildings it might be important, but she was not an architectural mage.

"Next question. If Vera has twelve apples and Tomas has six apples and Gertrude has less than..." Emma groaned. Not more word problems.

"YOU CALL THAT A SHIELD?" Professor Sesay scolded Richard. "There are so many holes in that shield I could call it swiss cheese!"

Richard blushed and redoubled his efforts, with Emma sensing him trying to plug the holes in the defensive shield he'd summoned during Defensive Magic 201. He was the only one she recognized in this class, with the rest of the students looking to be a few years younger than the two of them.

"Excellent form, Victor," he praised. "Judith, raise your shield faster or you'll be charred meat. Emma," he paused and sighed.

She braced herself for criticism.

"You have strength, I will give you that much. You can probably overpower most offensive spells just from your strength alone."

She allowed herself to grin.

The professor snapped his fingers and pointed his index finger at her face. "But that can lead to overconfidence." He chose that moment to attack her shield. It shattered. "Which can lead to distraction."

Emma's cheeks heated. *So much for being above reproach*, she thought. Yes, she was strong, but she was mostly untrained. That was the reason for this class though, wasn't it? "Yes, Professor," she said, knowing that was the answer he expected.

He sniffed anyway, as if doubting the sincerity of her response. "That is enough for the moment, class. Next we will focus on redirecting..."

"UNLIKE DEFENSIVE MAGIC," Professor Quaith said, walking back and forth in front of the class, his dark hair perfect, with not a hair out of place, "offensive magic requires you to be in a certain mindset. It is easy to defend yourself. You're being attacked, after all. Defense can come naturally in such circumstances. Or if friends or family are threatened, the need to defend them will rise up like a river after a heavy rain. But offensive magic, offensive magic is often used without provocation. It can be used for sneak attacks or to strike the first blow. It can be used to catch an enemy off balance and turn the tide of the battle before it even begins. It requires knowing that the cause you fight for, the cause that is prompting you to use offensive spells, is worth fighting for. Without conviction your spells will not zing as they should and you could easily lose the battle."

Emma shared a glance with Kylie. They were less than five minutes into Offensive Magic 101 and it was already far more intense than Defensive Magic had been.

"As some of you know, there are many different elements of existence. Each can be molded by a mage - some more easily than others depending on the mage - into spells. Every defensive spell arises from the need to counter an offensive spell. We will begin by describing the most basic single-element offensive spells, then move on to more complex multi-element spells..."

"CAN SOMEONE TELL ME what the author intended in this paragraph?" Professor Foster asked. Her long gray hair was tied back, and her green eyes searched the students' faces, as if trying to discern who knew the answer to her question.

Emma thought, then raised her hand. "He was describing the color of the curtains." *They were blue curtains, after all.*

"Yes, on the surface he was. Can someone else offer a more in-depth explanation?"

"The author was showing the inner mood of the character in the story through their in-depth description of the curtains."

"Excellent answer, Hadrian. That is correct. Rather than simply writing 'Joseph was sad,' the author described the blue nature of the curtains as a way of showing the sad nature of Joseph."

Emma rolled her eyes. They were just blue curtains, and conveniently, the author of the text they had been assigned to study was long dead and couldn't actually answer as to what their intent was. Of course the son of a queen would glean that from the text.

If this was all Language Arts 101 involved it was going to be a long class...

"DROP AND GIVE ME TWENTY!" Professor Kontos shouted at one of Emma's classmates. The boy's crime? He hadn't been standing straight enough.

In response, Emma stood as straight as she could, straining her back. She decided Physical Education was *not* fun. It wasn't that she was out of shape. She'd always eaten relatively healthy and played outside, not to mention traveling through the wilderness on the way to Tar Ebon. Yet, they were training to be mages, not soldiers. Why did they need this class? She wisely kept her face neutral so as to not reveal her inner thoughts.

Ethan, however, had no such compunction. Earlier that day he'd been forced to run laps around the indoor gymnasium their Physical Education class took place in after giving a snarky answer. Even now he was still running laps.

This is going to be a long class, she thought wearily.

Chapter 8

E mma awoke on her third day at the Tower and groaned as the ache in her muscles hit her. Physical Education was not fun.

Would you like me to ease the pain in your muscles? Shadow asked.

No, that's okay, Emma replied, stretching. When the pain goes away it will remind me of how far I've come.

As you wish. If the pain persists, I am always here.

Thanks, she replied sarcastically. Today was the weekend, however, which gave her two days to recover.

Emma changed and exited her room. She thought she had been up early, but the common room was already bustling with activity.

One of her roommates, Agnes, waved to her. "Emma!" She ran over. "Do you have any plans today?"

She thought hard. *Come on, think of something.* She could say she was sick. Or had a date. Or needed to study. All of those could get her caught in a lie, however, and she didn't want to lose Agnes as a friend - perhaps her only friend on her floor. "No," she had to admit at last. "I don't have any plans today. Why?"

"There's a big mageball game today that I thought you might like."

"What's mageball?" Emma asked, furrowing her brows.

Agnes' eyes went wide. "You don't know what mageball is? Now you'll have to come!"

Emma resisted the urge to roll her eyes. Why couldn't she have thought up a better response? She shrugged. "Okay, I'll go."

Agnes smiled wide and tugged at her arm. "Come on!" She led her out of the dorm and to the elevator. They went up several levels, farther than Emma remembered going, and emerged to the sight of amphitheater seating tapering down toward a field of some sort on the far side of the central shaft. They walked down a few rows and took a seat. It looked like they were on a balcony of some sort, for they were above the stone field, looking down. A hoop rose on a pillar at each end and a wooden statue sat atop a pedestal behind each hoop. One hoop was painted red, the other blue. A girl or boy in red or blue robes guarded the hoop of the matching color. A cheer rose from the crowd and from beneath the balcony a stream of a dozen students, half in red, half in blue, emerged. One member from each team met in the center where a man in black robes stood. They flipped something, a coin, Emma guessed, and the referee pointed to the red team.

"Red team is attacking, blue is defending," Agnes commented excitedly. "I know the captain of the blue team," she intimated in a whisper.

A ball of flame flared through the air above the stone floor. It arced toward the red hoop. It was halfway across the field before it dissipated. No sooner had the flame extinguished than another hurtled toward it. This time it split into three smaller balls of fire, each making a line toward the wooden statue behind each hoop.

"Let me guess," Emma said, "they have to burn the statue?"

"Yep. They have to use fire to burn the statue to earn points. But there are rules. They can't just ignite the statue directly, they have to use a ball of heat. And the other team can block or use other magic to distract the casters. The offending team's goal is to confound the defending team so much that they can't stop the ball of fire."

"I don't see any other spells being used?"

"Just wait. The match just started. That was the opening salvo."

"How long does the match last?"

"Each team is on offense for twenty minutes, known as a quarter." She pointed to an hourglass tucked into an alcove against the wall opposite the balcony. "There are four quarters. So each team is on offense two times. Each time they ignite the statue, even if they don't burn it to ash, earns them a point. If a team manages to turn the statue to ash they automatically win."

Indeed, the next attempt was far more complicated. With her eyes alone she saw lightning, ice, fire and rocks being flung toward the defending side. The defenders seemed to combat the attacks with ease.

Wearing them down, Emma guessed. *Or testing to see which element they responded slowest to?* She didn't dare ask Agnes, lest the quarter be over before she finished answering.

The next salvo prompted Emma to watch not with her eyes but with her magic. She sensed the elements raging above the field below and could see where the confusion could come into play. With so many elements flying around, in defense and offense, it was impossible for one person to keep track. She locked on to the signature of heat suggesting a fire ball as it neared the defenders hoop. The goal-keeper, acting as the last line of defense, held off countering the attack until the last moment, deflecting the ball into the ground.

The goal-keepers conserve their energy as long as possible to avoid being tired out during the battle. Fighting for forty minutes would be a long time, even with a break in-between.

A maelstrom created by the offense swirled toward the defenders hoop. It looked like a red, white and yellow with hints of gray whirlwind. The defenders chipped away at it, but their efforts only slowed it. As it neared the goal-keeper they attacked it but were forced to leap out of the way as the whirlwind of death passed through the hoop and engulfed the statue. Fire from within started to burn the statue.

Instead of attacking the maelstrom, the defenders changed tactics and attacked the offending players. A ball of ice slammed into one attacker, breaking their concentration, while a hail of rocks peppered a pair of attackers. With each offending player distracted the whirlwind weakened and finally died away. The wooden statue was charred, and one of its arms fell off as Emma watched, but it was still standing.

I guess this isn't so bad, Emma thought. It trained mages how to think on their feet, how to work as a team and, probably, how to fight in real life with magic. She settled in to watch the rest of the game.

The remainder of the first quarter passed without further incident and left both sides looking exhausted. A five-minute intermission allowed for them to eat and drink on the sidelines before they were back on their feet for the second period. The previous defenders gave as good as they'd gotten and by the end of period two the enemy statue was down to its waist.

The third period had just begun when a shadowy mist appeared from nowhere. That made Emma, who had been leaning back watching the crowd during intermission, sit up straight. None of the teams had used anything like this yet. Was it a new spell? The shadows coalesced into the silhouette of a faceless man.

"Your school is doomed!" the figure's deep voice boomed, echoing through the cavernous arena. The crowd started chattering, while the players backed away to the hoops. "Flee now before death and destruction rains down upon you in the name of Rae'Shela!" The shadowy figure burst apart and faded smoke from a campfire caught in the wind.

The referee came out, clearly shaken, and amplified his voice. "The match is canceled," he spluttered, "all students are to return to their dormitories at once and await further instructions."

"Has anything like this ever happened before?" Emma asked Agnes.

Her haunted eyes held the answer. "Never."

The two did not speak as they rode a crowded elevator down to their floor and re-entered their dorm. The common room was packed with students, all talking in low voices. Had they all seen the same shadowy figure? Her question was answered minutes later when Professor Quaith entered the dorm, out of breath and puffing. "Everyone remain calm," he said, then cleared his throat. "I'm telling you girls first, then I'll see to the boys. The staff are looking into the intrusion that was witnessed on multiple levels of the Tower. All students are to remain calm but remain in the dormitory while we search the Tower from top-to-bottom. The prefects will be in charge in the interim. Does everyone understand?" He waited until most of the students, including Emma, were nodding their agreement. "Good." He gave a stiff nod to Kyra and swept out of the dorm - no doubt on the way to say the same thing to the boys.

Emma made for her room, but Kyra intercepted her. "Where are you going?" she demanded.

"To my room." She looked imploringly at Agnes, but the scrawny Gallean girl continued on, not wanting to tangle with the prefect. "What's it to you?"

"You stood up for Isabelle the other day. I didn't properly pay you back for that."

Where was Isabelle, anyway? Emma glanced around the room but didn't see her iconic scowl or dark clothing anywhere. Wasn't the Tower on lockdown?

"No need to thank me."

"Oh, I'm not thanking you. I want to challenge you to a duel."

"A duel?" Emma asked incredulously. "Why?"

"You need to be taught a lesson. How to not disrespect a prefect."

The rational part of Emma's brain said to walk away and ignore the comment. Or to tell Professor Quaith and let him quash the matter. But the angry part of her brain, the part inherited from her mother, got angry. Her face burned. "Teach me a lesson? Oh, it's on. Name the time and place." *I will tear you up*, Emma thought.

"Tonight, at twenty-two bells."

That was two hours past curfew. "Deal. Where?"

"Hmmm," she stroked her chin. "The mageball arena."

"I'll be there."

Kyra smirked. "No blabbing to your friends, no teachers and no cheating. Deal?"

Emma glared at her. "Deal."

The two went their separate ways, with Kyra going off to scold some first years about their clothing and Emma returning to her room. She passed Isabelle in the hall. The assassin's daughter was exiting the privy and only gave Emma an impassive glance as she passed, though she did nod. *I suppose that's better than a hostile glare*, Emma thought. Now to prepare for the duel that evening.

Chapter 9

The twenty-first hour had come and gone before Emma left her sleeping roommates behind and made her way out to the common room. She reached for the door knob.

"Where are you going?"

Emma jerked and spun. Isabelle stood there, hood down but still wearing her signature black clothing. *Doesn't she own anything other than black clothing?* "Isabelle, you scared me."

"That was the idea. Where are you going?"

"What's it matter to you?"

Isabelle shrugged. "It doesn't. But I saw Kyra leaving a little while ago, and now here you go...after curfew...leaving to some unknown place. Seems like an awfully big coincidence to me." She locked eyes with Emma.

Emma's shoulders slumped. "Okay. I'm not supposed to tell anyone, but Kyra challenged me to a duel."

"To the death?"

"No," Emma said hesitantly. *At least, I hope not.*

"Then it's not a real duel."

"What do you know about real duels?" Emma snapped, before realizing who she was talking to.

"I'm the daughter of an assassin, remember?"

"That doesn't mean you are an assassin. And isn't she a *former* assassin?"

Isabelle shrugged infuriatingly again. "You don't unlearn how to be an assassin. Why don't you let me come along with you to this duel?"

"She said come alone."

96

"Of course she did. And how do you know she won't stab you in the back and throw you out a window once she has you alone? You need someone like me."

"To protect me from being stabbed in the back? Or to stab me in the back yourself?"

"I don't have any quarrels with you," Isabelle said.

"You could have fooled me. The way you were glaring at me on your parents' ship says otherwise."

Isabelle adopted an annoyed expression. "We don't have time for this right now. You need to get going or you're going to be late for your duel."

"No," Emma stood her ground. "You might not have a quarrel with me, but you do have a problem with me. What is it?"

The girl sighed. "Fine, if you really want to do this right now. I think you're entitled and have too big of a head."

Emma stepped back as if slapped. "What makes you think that?"

"When my parents got back to the ship all they could talk about was you. You and your power. You and your brother holding back an entire army of mages until reinforcements arrived."

"We had help from the Staff of Agamar," Emma protested. "We're not that powerful." She neglected to mention Shadow and the help he had given her while holding the staff. An ordinary mage would have been corrupted as quickly as Alivia had. "So that's it, you're jealous?"

Isabelle said nothing but diverted her eyes to the floor.

"I'm right," Emma deduced. "You are jealous that your parents came to help us and you didn't get to come along. When they got back, you felt your parents were prouder of us than they were of you. Am I close?"

The girl flicked her eyes up and glared before again studying the floor.

"You wish they would talk about you like that. Which is why you want so badly to prove yourself." It wasn't a question.

"Do you know how hard it is being the daughter of a 'famous' assassin?" Isabelle asked in a fierce whisper, making a quoting gesture when saying famous and meeting Emma's eyes. "The looks I get? The assumptions about me? The daughter of the most powerful assassin in the world and one of the most powerful mages must be great in her own right. That puts a lot of pressure on me."

"Oh," Emma said, her smug smile evaporating. Isabelle brought up a point Emma hadn't considered before. Her parents might have been semi-famous in Ironforge, but outside of their sleepy town they were nothing. She couldn't imagine being the daughter of famous mages and the pressure that would bring with it. Would she want to be? "I'm sorry. I hadn't thought of that."

Isabelle sniffed and rolled her eyes. "Yeah, most people don't." She wiped her eyes, suggesting she had been crying, though Emma couldn't see her face well in the dim light of the common room at night. "Now that I'm done pouring my heart out, are you ready to go?"

"You still want to come with me?"

"I meant what I said. I'll watch your back. If you trust me." Her last sentence suggested that might no longer be the case.

Did Emma trust Isabelle? A day earlier and she would have said no. But she didn't have another choice. She couldn't contact Kylie without running into a prefect or alerting other students, and although she could contact Ethan through the link there was still the risk he would be caught by the boys' prefect, Trevor. She found she sympathized with Isabelle, even if she didn't trust her yet. "Alright, you can come with me."

The two exited the dorm of House Longclaw and made for the stairs. Emma felt that using the elevator at night could alert any professors or night watchmen to the presence of students up and about. Did they have night security at the Tower? She hadn't asked and didn't want to find out. They made their way up several flights of stairs until they reached the floor housing the arena. She found herself stepping out in a shadowy hall beneath the balcony she had sat at earlier that day before the ghost or spirit or whatever it was had appeared. She still didn't know what that thing had been. It had appeared on every floor, so clearly it hadn't been a mass hallucination. What could it have been? She didn't believe in ghosts, and her parents told her believing in such things was silly, but what did her parents know? Could the soul of a poor mage have been trapped in the walls somehow? But why wait until now to show itself?

Her musings were interrupted as she reached the arena. Isabelle stopped short of the entrance. "I'll wait back here, in the shadows," she said.

"Can you disappear like your mother?" Emma asked.

"No," Isabelle said tightly. "Not yet, anyway. My father taught me what magic he could, but my mother couldn't teach me what she knew."

"Okay. Wish me luck."

"It's not to the death, but good luck anyway," Isabelle replied.

"Thanks." Emma stepped out into the arena.

Kyra stood to Emma's right, at the foot of the pole holding up a hoop. Her red hair was tied back and she scowled as she caught sight of Emma. "So you decided to show up? Did you come alone?"

"Yes," Emma called back. "You?" she made a show of looking around the vast arena, then walking to the center and looking up toward the balcony. No one anywhere that she could see. *If she was going to ambush me her cohorts wouldn't be standing in plain sight though, would they?* She didn't think so, but it hadn't hurt to check.

"Of course. I am a woman of dignity," she responded.

Emma snorted but kept her retort to herself. "What are the rules of this duel?"

"Anything goes. The first person to surrender loses and has to do anything the winner says."

Anything? That wouldn't be good. *All the more incentive for me to win.* "I agree."

"Excellent." She smiled wide. "Go to that end and we'll begin."

Emma was halfway to the opposite end of the arena when she felt magic building from Kyra's end. She spun, drawing upon her magic immediately, and felt her foe already unleashing a wave of intense heat toward her. It caused the air to shimmer instead of burn, but Emma had no doubt it could cause serious damage to her body. A flashback to being burned by her twin brother rose in her mind and it took an effort to suppress it. *Focus on the present*, she scolded herself. She rushed to throw up a latticework of defense to disperse the heat. She formed the lattice of strings of air with the intent of siphoning the heat like the pipes under Ironforge did back home. With any luck, the heat would not affect her or at least not burn her skin.

Indeed, the wave of heat met her air tube construct and washed through the tubes of air forged by Emma'a mind. She could see the heat washing toward the walls, floor and ceiling of the arena, allowing only a small amount of heat to continue on toward her. In the end, the heat that reached her was no more powerful than a summer breeze. Emma smirked. Was that the best she could do?

Kyra didn't seem to react physically, but the delay before she tried another spell told Emma she was shocked.

Emma took advantage of the gap to prepare her own attack. Though Kyra had not technically cheated, she had struck first before Emma was ready, which in Emma's mind was sort of cheating. The rational part of her brain told her that true enemies wouldn't wait - they would attack when Emma least expected it. She ignored the logical voice and summoned lightning. Lightning was a difficult element to manipulate due to its ephemeral nature, with only few mages being able to control it effectively. Or so Alivia had said. Emma had learned within a day of being at the Tower that Alivia's nickname had been "Lightning O'Leary" and she suspected it was with good reason.

The ball of lightning grew between her palms, soon reaching a diameter of a meter or more. She cast it toward Kyra, not expecting it to actually strike the girl.

Indeed, Kyra seemed almost cocky in her response to the lightning ball. She waited until the ball was within a few feet of her before holding out her hands and stopping the spell. But the distraction was what Emma had been waiting for.

While Kyra was focusing on controlling the lightning ball, Emma evacuated the heat out of a thin space in front of her, making it frigid. She cast the thin rectangle of cold air forward and continued to chill the air in the line behind the rectangle. The result was a beam of cold air barreling toward Kyra. Indeed, it caught her foe off-guard as it blew through the lightning orb and struck Kyra in the chest. She flew backward and slammed into the physical wall with an audible oof.

Fear struck Emma in that moment. Fear that Kyra might be hurt, or worse, dead. She watched for sign of movement, regretting her dirty tactic. She hadn't thought it was that dirty, though, considering Kyra was a prefect and Emma was technically a first-year student.

Kyra stirred and stood, her face bright red. "You'll pay for that!" She roared. She followed words with action a moment later by hurling fire, ice and lightning toward Emma, encased in wind. Rocks also rose from the ground all around the arena and barreled toward Emma.

The first-year mage could barely react to the main attack while under the constant barrage of tiny rocks peppering her. At the last moment she threw up a barrier of air, but it wasn't enough. Kyra's spell overwhelmed her defense and this time it was *her* flying backward, pain wracking her body.

I have initiated emergency repair procedures, she distantly heard Shadow say in her mind.

Thanks, Emma thought in reply, groaning through her mouth as her entire body burned with pain. She looked down and saw her clothing actually *was* on fire. Panic set in and she hurriedly drained the heat away, but she did it improperly and her body warmed, causing her to become even further distressed.

She saw a figure emerge from the side hallway and for a moment couldn't identify them. Then it hit her. Isabelle. She had come as backup for Emma in the event she got into trouble. *No*, Emma thought, *don't show yourself now*, but it was too late. This technically hadn't been treachery, and she could lose the duel now for breaking the rule of not bringing anyone with her. She supposed she could claim Isabelle had followed her without her knowledge, but she doubted Kyra would buy that excuse.

"Emma!" Isabelle shouted as she knelt beside the wounded girl. She clearly saw something that gave her heart, for she said, "Good, you're alive. Can you speak?"

"Have...to...stand," Emma struggled to speak. "Must...finish."

"No, just lie back. Your need to rest."

"Cheater!" Kyra called. "You will forfeit this duel for that."

"Shut your mouth!" Isabelle roared, turning on the girl and embracing her magic. It swirled around her like a tempest, waiting to be unleashed. Her father was said to be a powerful air and water mage, and the way the wind swirled around her suggested it was true. Idly, as she tried to ignore the pain, Emma thought that wind magic would be useful while sailing the seas.

"Do you surrender?" Kyra asked, ignoring Isabelle and readying another spell.

Yes, Emma wanted to say. Desperately wanted to say. "I..."

"What is the meaning of this?" A voice boomed from the mouth of the hallway. Alivia O'Leary stood there, resplendent despite wearing a nightgown. She held no magic, but then, she didn't need to considering the fact any student stupid enough to attack her wouldn't last an instant.

Emma groaned, this time more from embarrassment than from the pain. Did Shadow have something to numb the emotions? He had said he did, but Emma wasn't sure if this warranted a measure so drastic. She attempted instead to stand and managed to come to a shaky position leaning against the wall.

"Arch mage," Kyra began.

"Do not speak. I see everything I need to see. Illegal dueling." It was a statement of fact. "Both of you, to my office, now!"

"What about me?" Isabelle asked, actually appearing to be cowed by the arch mage.

"You are to return to your dormitory. Professor Quaith will deal with you in the morning for being out of bed so late and for aiding and abetting your friend."

Isabelle nodded, apparently not willing to argue with someone who could probably fry her in an instant. She cast one last glance at Emma, a glance that suggested she was sorry to be leaving, before walking toward the entrance to the arena and disappearing a moment later.

Emma limped toward Alivia, feeling better with each step. Whatever procedures Shadow had implemented were taking affect it seemed. She glared at Kyra, who limped herself. Maybe they'd each given as good as they got.

Alivia led the two errant duelists out of the arena and to the elevator. She led them up several floors and then to her office. She stopped at the door. "Kyra first." The girl entered and Emma was left to sit on a bench outside.

Several minutes later, despite hearing no raised voices from within, the door opened and Kyra came out, looking chastised with her head down and eyes studying the floor tiles as she exited without a word. Emma turned back to see Alivia standing in the doorway. She beckoned with a finger. Emma followed her inside. The office was decorated sparsely, with no personal portraits on the desk and only landscape paintings occupying the walls. She took a seat across from Alivia.

For several moments, the arch mage stared hard at Emma and did not speak. This caused the girl to squirm in discomfort. What was she going to say to her? Would she yell or scream? She couldn't imagine a particularly good outcome.

"Why?" Was her first question.

Why what? Emma thought. Why had she agreed to it? Why had she damaged Kyra so much? Why had she brought Isabelle along? She assumed it was the first question. "She challenged me and..."

"And what? You couldn't say no?" Her voice sounded as though she were straining to keep calm. It was a tone Emma knew well from when she would do something bad back in Ironforge. It never ended well.

"There's this boy," Emma began, deciding to try a different tactic. "Kyra claims he's hers, and I sort of like him and..."

"So you couldn't say no *and* it was all over a boy?" She asked incredulously. "You risked bodily harm - no, death - over a silly crush on a boy?"

When she put it like that, it did seem quite silly. "Kyra has hated me from the moment I stepped into the Tower. I wanted to put her in her place."

"So there it is. You let hate and anger rule you and wanted to prove you were more powerful than her." It was not a question.

Emma nodded. She was right.

Alivia sighed. "Can I tell you a story?"

"Of course," Emma stammered, though in her mind she really wished she could be released to flee from the office.

"Twenty years ago, perhaps twenty-one years now, the world was threatened by the Krai'kesh. You're familiar with them, are you not?"

Emma nodded. "My parents told me stories of them. It all ended on the Fields of Pelinor, right?"

"So the world was told," Alivia said. "But in truth, some Krai'kesh had been left as a rearguard. They were not involved in the battle and fled north after their commander was killed."

Emma gasped. "Are they still up there?" Her mind flashed to the image of another great Krai'kesh invasion, the city of Tar Ebon and surrounding countryside burning at their advance.

"No. The Eternals, along with several surviving mages, went north and destroyed their progenitor pods, effectively stopping them from breeding more of their kind. Still some escaped and scattered into the world."

"I'm sorry, but what does that..."

"What does that have to do with you?" Alivia asked, arching an eyebrow. "The next part does. After the Krai'kesh scattered, dissension grew in the Tower. Dark mages, followers of the Krai'kesh god Rae'Shela, attempted to seize the Tower. They challenged the Eternals and myself, for I had been placed in a position of power after the arch mages of the Tower died in an earlier battle with the Krai'kesh, to duels. The stakes were high, but the side of good prevailed and the dissenters were cast out."

"Why didn't you imprison them?"

Alivia sighed. "Our mistake was so obvious even a sixteen-year-old girl can see it," she said, more to herself than Emma. "We thought showing mercy to them would change their minds. That by sparing their freedom and their lives they would see the light and return to the side of good. We realized too late they were beyond redemption. The Cult of Rae was born the day those thirteen dark mages were exiled from the Tower. It spread like a plague, with disciples popping up around the world. The Rakosh Empire was hit particularly hard by the infestation of fanatics, prompting the emperor to declare a religious crusade that even to this day is spreading across his continent. But that is a tale for another day. Needless to say, there are times to fight, times to duel, when the stakes are real. But this," she waved her hand, "fighting over a boy. Fighting over *pride*. It does no one any good. I would have expected more from you, Emma. I know your parents raised you better than this."

Shame warred with anger inside Emma. Anger not at Alivia, but at herself. She was right - her parents had raised her better than this. "I'm sorry," was all that felt right to say in the moment.

"You must of course be punished for this transgression," Alivia said. "The other professors would have my job if they suspected I was showing favoritism. Several of the cellars below the Tower are in desperate need of organization and dusting. You will be assigned to work down there. You and Kyra, together. And I will strongly suggest to Professor Quaith that Isabelle be included in the work crew for sneaking out and her complicit nature."

Emma stifled a groan and nodded slowly. Any punishment was fair and well-earned, even if it would be tedious. She didn't dare ask how long the punishment would be for.

"Now go on, get out of here. Get a good night's sleep and report to Professor McGarvon tomorrow on floor B3."

Emma nodded, committing the professor's name to memory. He or she did not sound familiar to Emma, though to be fair she had only been at the Tower three days. "Thank you, Arch Mage," she said formally.

Alivia smiled kindly. "A good talent, that. Knowing when to address another by their title and when to address them by their name."

Emma took her leave silently and returned to the dorm. When she entered, Kyra was sitting in the chair. The girl looked up and it appeared she'd been crying. "I'm sorry," Emma said. Alivia hadn't strictly told her to apologize, but it felt right. It was what her mother and father would have wanted her to do.

Kyra sniffled but didn't speak for a long moment. Long enough that Emma started to eye the hallway leading to her bedroom, intending to leave without hearing the girls reply. At last she spoke. "You think you're so much better than everyone. But you aren't. Doom will come up on the Tower and soon you will be groveling at *my* feet!" She stood up and stormed off to her bedroom.

Emma blinked, taken aback by the ferocity of the reply from Kyra. *What was all that about?* Doom coming upon the Tower? That sounded eerily similar to what the shadow figure had said during the mageball match today. Maybe Kyra was just repeating what she'd heard in an attempt to cow Emma? Well, if that was the case, Emma refused to be cowed into submission again. They had met on the proverbial field of battle and come to a stalemate. While Emma had no intention of fighting the prefect again, she vowed that if she *did* she would be prepared.

Chapter 10

"What in the name of the Founders were you thinking?" Professor Quaith demanded. His flushed cheeks and narrowed eyes stood in stark contrast to the jovial professor Emma had met only days earlier. His eyes flicked between the three girls, though Emma could have sworn he focused more on Isabelle and her than on Kyra.

"Professor," Emma began. "We weren't going to hurt each other." She looked down under his glare. "Or at least we didn't intend to."

"You nearly *killed* each other *and* got caught by an arch mage. Could you have been any more foolish to go out the same night as an intrusion into the Tower?"

Emma perked up at that. She hadn't heard it called an intrusion. The term she'd heard repeated by the gossip mill was "haunting" or "ghost." She opened her mouth to speak - to ask more about the intrusion - but the professor continued over her.

"Do not speak. I don't need to know the reason, and I fear you opening your mouth could prove me wrong in my estimation of your foolishness."

Emma's cheeks burned, in part from embarrassment and partly from anger. There was no need to insult them like that. It had been a mistake, yes. Potentially a deadly mistake, but they were students. That had to be expected, didn't it?

He sighed. "I suppose I should expect nothing less from teenage girls. What do you have to say for yourself, Kyra?"

Kyra kept her mouth closed for several long seconds, but something in the man's tone of voice, or the look he gave her, convinced her to speak. "I regret going out tonight to duel."

"And you?" he asked Isabelle.

"I just followed my friend," she challenged. "I didn't engage in the duel."

"No, but you did break curfew and failed to notify the proper authorities of the duel about to take place. Let me ask you - if every girl in the Tower jumped from the roof, would you?"

Isabelle snorted. "Of course not. I'm not stupid."

"And yet you followed the stupid actions of a fellow teenage girl without question," he again pointed at Emma.

"Maybe if you chose better prefects that didn't pick fights with first year students you wouldn't have had this problem."

Emma thought the professor couldn't get any angrier. She was wrong.

Magic crackled around him and it seemed like he would incinerate Isabelle on the spot. "Why you insolent..."

"Professor," Kyra snapped in a sharp tone.

The feeling of magic faded and the professor shook his head. Instead of scolding Kyra for her tone, he instead pointed at the door. "You all may go, now. Report to Professor McGarvon immediately. And you're lucky Arch Mage O'Leary assigned this punishment. I would not have been so lenient." That last bit seemed intended to re-assert his power, after being scolded by the prefect.

What is going on between the professor and Kyra? Emma wondered. For him to accept such a commanding tone from Kyra and not say anything bothered her.

PROFESSOR MCGARVON eyed the three girls from above the spectacles that seemed supported by the tip of her nose alone. Her gray hair was pinned up in a bun. "So, the three of you are to assist me as punishment, eh?" She asked as if she hadn't known their crime.

Emma nodded, but her companions remained where they were. Isabelle stood straight as a sword with her expression calm while Kyra looked like she was clenching her teeth.

"Well, don't just stand here. You'll start by dusting the rooms from top to bottom, then mopping and finally organizing books on the shelves." She pointed to a multiple stacks of books in various states of disarray behind her. "The dusters are in the closet, over there. And no magic," she pointed at each of them in turn. "If I sense so much as a wind spell you'll get double your sentence."

Emma stifled a groan. They'd already been sentenced to come down here and work every weekend for two months. She really didn't want to stretch that to a third of a year.

Kyra made no attempt to hide her groan. "I am a prefect. I don't want to work next to these first years."

Professor McGarvon was not amused but smirked anyway. "All right. If you're too good to dust and mop, you can have a different task." She paused for dramatic effect. "You can clean the privies down here. Students have been known to come down to the basement levels to hide the 'shame' of their particularly," her face twisted in mock disgust, "gruesome bowel movements."

Kyra's eyes went wide with shock. "The privies. But I..."

"You what?" a dangerous tone had entered the professor's voice now. "You're too good to do work as part of your punishment? If that's the case, perhaps I should send you back up to Arch Mage O'Leary and have her deal with you? Would you like that? I'm sure she can find a more suitable punishment for your...delicate nature."

Emma snickered.

The professor's eyes switched in an instant. "Is something funny?"

Emma straightened further. "No, ma'am." It was a mistake to think this professor, though she looked like a kindly grandmother, was kind. She seemed to have a spine of steel.

"Good. Just remember you got yourselves into this mess. Thus you've got no one to blame but yourselves." She clapped her hands. "Get to it before I march you back upstairs."

Kyra stalked out of the large chamber, while Emma and Isabelle went to the broom closet and pulled out a pair of dusters.

"Grab a broom, too," the professor said. "You'll need to sweep the floor before mopping."

"Yes, ma'am," Emma said. She grabbed two brooms and handed one to Isabelle.

Isabelle didn't speak until they were out in the hallway with no one around. "I've swabbed the decks before, but this is humiliating."

"It's only fair," Emma pointed out. "We did the crime, we do the time."

"All because you convinced me to go down there."

"I didn't convince you of anything," Emma said, hoping the girl was joking. "I didn't *want* you to come with me, or have you forgotten?"

"I know, I know. It's just...my second day here and I'm already getting in trouble. What will my parents say?"

"I don't know them very well," Emma ventured, "but your father seems pretty cool about things like that and what you did sounds like something your mother would do."

"I guess." She smiled. "Hey, maybe when we're done cleaning we can duel." She brandished the feather duster like a sword and the broom like a spear."

Emma chuckled. "With our luck you'll poke my eye out and I'll end up tickling you to death."

The two girls entered the first archive room. The way Emma understood it, the sub-levels of the Tower were filled with books and other documents, along with machinery that operated the advanced features of the Tower. She had yet to see any sign of said machinery, but what she stared at now was row upon row of bound books and scrolls on bookshelves that rose a dozen feet or more. A ladder on wheels leaned against each bookshelf. Emma ran to one, jumped on and felt the ladder sliding effortlessly in the direction she'd been going. She felt the wind in her hair for a brief moment before friction, and her weight, slowed it down. She looked to Isabelle, who just smirked.

They settled into a rhythm that involved them each taking a side of the room and methodically dusting the bookshelves from top to bottom while re-organizing the books into some semblance of order. Then, once the dust had been swept from its perch, they set about sweeping it into dustpans. Isabelle ran to fetch the mop and bucket. "You want to fill it?" Isabelle asked.

"Sure," Emma said. She took the bucket and headed toward the privies, which she could smell and which also were designated by a sign. She paused outside the girls' privy. She heard voices within. One sounded like Kyra, which made sense, but the other...a man?

"Why should I forgive you for your failing?" the voice asked. It was a deep voice that tickled Emma's memory. A moment later it clicked. The shadowy man from the day before. It sounded just like him! Emma's breath caught in her throat. What was Kyra doing talking to him?"

"I would have ended her if the arch mage hadn't intervened. I don't know how she was tipped off."

"I do not have time for your excuses. The plan is almost ready to be implemented. She must be out of the way."

"Why is she so important?" Kyra challenged.

"Shhh...do you hear that?"

Emma froze. Had they heard her in the hallway? She didn't think she'd made any noise. Still, she held her breath.

"No," Kyra said quizzically.

"That is the deadly sound of silence that will follow the next time you dare to question me. Find a way to take her out of the equation soon or I will take my displeasure out on you." A swooshing sound followed his words and Emma got the distinct sense he had disappeared.

Feeling brave, Emma crept forward and peeked around the corner. Kyra held an orb in her hand. It possessed the same swirling inky pattern of the orb she'd seen at Senegal Fortress had. So she had a communication orb? *Time to go.* She turned and walked as quickly as she could back the way she'd come and slipped back into the room where Isabelle continued to sweep.

The girl looked up. "Why is the bucket empty?" Then, seeing the fear in Emma's eyes, she asked, "What's wrong? What happened?"

"I overheard Kyra talking to someone. A man. He talked about a plan and killing me and Kyra is working for him and..."

"Whoa, hold up," Isabelle said, stepping up to her and putting her hands on her shoulders. "Calm down. Take some deep breaths and start from the beginning."

Emma did as instructed, closing her eyes and taking deep breaths while counting to ten. At last she opened them and met Isabelle's intense but concerned gaze. "So I went down to..." she recounted the tale over the next several minutes.

Isabelle was silent for several moments after Emma finished. "So you think she's with the Cult of Rae?"

Emma shook her head. "I honestly don't know if the shadowy guy is with the Cult of Rae. But I do know they aren't up to anything good."

"And they're targeting you?"

"It sounded like it. They talked about Alivia interrupting the duel as if she stopped something."

"Then why don't we go tell Alivia?"

"We don't have any proof. Yeah, she was talking to someone, but I didn't see him."

"So? At least warn her so she can keep a better eye on Kyra."

"No. Not until I know more. You and I will keep an eye on her."

Isabelle gave her a dubious look. "I have a bad feeling about this, and I'm used to sailing through storms on my father's ship. But I'll ride out this storm and wait to see if we make it out the other side."

"Thank you," Emma said, thankful for the confidence her friend was placing in her. "But now I want to find someplace else to get water for this." She hefted the bucket.

"There's got to be another privy down here. Come on, I'll go with you."

The two left the archive room and walked past the privy where Kyra was working. The sub-levels of the Tower were a warren of tunnels with passageways running in multiple directions and countless doors lining the corridors.

Emma stopped after losing track of the turns they'd made. "Are we lost?" she asked.

"I don't know," Isabelle admitted. "It's only my third day here, remember?"

"I'm only a day more senior than you," Emma pointed out. "Whose idea was it to find another privy? We should have just went and asked Professor McGarvon."

"We could call for help."

"We might be too far out for that."

Isabelle shrugged. "It's that or stay here till we starve."

"Let's not get dramatic." Isabelle had a point, however. "Maybe I can sense the privy. There has to be another one around here." That was the theory behind their entire trip, after all. She drew upon her magic and felt her consciousness float above her body. She could feel the stone composing the walls and see the space between the bricks. She followed the path of the hallway with her mind and turned the corner. She was able to "see" what lay around the corner - in an elemental sense, anyway. She could see the torches in their braziers and the flows of air. If she concentrated she could sense the droplets of water in the air. She stretched her mind further, peeking into rooms as she went, but they were all the same. Books and dust ad nauseum. But that changed when she turned one particular corner.

A glow which reminded her of the sun in magical terms emanated from beneath a door at the end of the hallway. *What is that?* Emma thought. She floated her consciousness closer. She sensed the presence of humans, guards, most likely, and the metal of the door. She pressed her corporeal hand against the metal and tried to press against it, seeking entry. Her way was blocked. She could not sense what lay beyond the door.

Evidently, her intrusion, or attempted intrusion, drew the attention of the guards. A moment later she felt two unknown presences drawing upon magic and felt her own senses being repulsed, as if she were being driven down the hallway. Back she was pushed until she finally let go of her magic and opened her eyes.

"Did you find the privy?" Isabelle asked hopefully.

"No," Emma said, swallowing.

Footsteps echoed in the distance. Moments later two guards turned the corner, swords in one hand and a ball of flame in the other. "Halt!" one of them called.

"What did you do?" Isabelle demanded.

"I don't know for sure," Emma offered. Had she reached a restricted part of the Tower? The presence of guards suggested she had. "Hello," she said to the guards while offering a half-smile.

The guards were not amused. "Who are you?"

"I am Emma. I'm a first-year student. This is Isabelle, she's a first-year student also."

"What are you doing down here?"

"Funny story. We were trying to find a privy to fill this." She hefted the bucket. "We're serving time down here cleaning out archive rooms as punishment. You can ask Professor McGarvon for confirmation."

"There's a privy right by the professor's office," the second guard pointed out. "So what are you doing this far into the sub-levels?"

"And this close to the core," the first guard added.

"Core? I don't know anything about a core. I stretched out my mind to try to find the privy faster. We didn't go to the first privy because it was being cleaned." She was babbling, she knew, but she felt they needed to know the facts before they roasted them. They still held their flame and blades at the ready. "I didn't mean anything by the intrusion."

The guards continued to glare at her for a long moment, their eyes independently flicking between the two girls. At last the first guard sighed, sheathed his sword and extinguished his fire. "I can show you to another privy." He nodded to his companion. "You go back to the door."

The second guard nodded and trotted off, the flame extinguishing but the sword still clutched in his hand.

"Follow me," the remaining guard said, beckoning them. He led them back the way he'd come but turned left at the turn instead of right. There, at the end of a dead-end hallway, they found the privy. "Here you are. I trust you can fill your bucket and find your way back without hand-holding?"

Emma flushed, her cheeks burning. If she hadn't been in the wrong she would have bit out a remark. As it was, she had to shoot Isabelle a sharp glance to forestall her making a biting comment. "We can find our way back from here." *I hope.* "Thank you for your assistance."

The guard grunted and went back the way he'd come.

The girls went inside and Emma placed the bucket below the tap and turned on the water while Isabelle held the mop. The plumbing in the Tower was far beyond what they'd had in Ironforge. Back home, water had been ferried from the fountains to their homes, with no personal plumbing in the house. Here, pipes went through the walls, ceiling and floors and carried water to even the highest levels of the Tower. Emma still wasn't quite sure how the technology worked, though she was sure she could ask Shadow. She didn't have time for the sometimes-annoying voice in her head to lecture her on how stuff worked, however.

"So did you really swab the decks of your father's ship?" Emma asked as water sprayed into the bucket.

"Yes. I wasn't a spoiled brat. I had to do chores and help the crew, the same as anyone. I had to work harder, actually, since Mother insisted on teaching me to fight and Father insisted on teaching me magic and science."

Emma scrunched her nose up. "How did you find time in the day for all that?"

"Quite easily. It's boring on a ship at sea, really. You get tired of seeing nothing but open ocean for miles around, so you go below decks where all there is to do is read a book or talk. But books get tiresome and conversations run dry. Training, in magic and martial techniques, helped to stave off the boredom."

Emma hefted the water bucket. "We better get this back." Professor McGarvon would not be happy if they didn't mop at least one of the archive chambers before the day ended.

Chapter 11

Emma awoke to darkness. The last thing she remembered was passing out in her bed after a hard day of dusting, organizing and mopping archive rooms. Now something, or someone, had awoken her.

"Emma," a voice whispered in the dark.

"Who is it?" Emma asked, fear constricting her throat. Would someone there to kidnap or murder her call out her name? That would be a pretty strange way to kidnap her. Unless the other girls in her room were already incapacitated and they wanted to toy with her. *Stop letting your imagination run away with you. You recognize that voice. It's Isabelle.* Indeed, as her mind woke up she recognized her friend's voice. "Isabelle?" she asked, just to be sure.

She felt a presence next to her, sensing the inhalation and exhalation from the assassin's daughter. "Something is wrong with me."

"What?" Emma asked, throwing off the covers. "Move out of the way." She swung her legs over the side of the bed and felt her bare feet touch the stone. One of the things she'd had to become accustomed to was bare stone floors. Back home she'd had bare wood floors, true, but there had been rugs galore and the feel of wood was different from the feel of stone. The advantage was that she could not get splinters from stone. As her eyes adjusted to the gloom she could make out the silhouette of Isabelle. Behind her, faint light given off by the candles in the hallway glowed from beneath the doorway, providing limited illumination to the room she shared with the other three mages in training.

"Follow me," Isabelle said, before heading toward the door.

Emma hesitated. Was she decent, or did she need a robe? No, she'd fallen asleep in her clothing, she reminded herself. She rose and followed Isabelle, her head feeling light for a moment as blood rushed from her head down into the rest of her body.

Isabelle padded silently down the hallway and led Emma to the common area. Through the large window, Emma could see that the sun was perhaps an hour from sunrise. Isabelle sat down on one of the couches and gestured for Emma to sit next to her. She wore a worried look on her face.

"What is it?" Emma asked again. She was worried for Isabelle, friend or no. What was wrong with her?"

"I woke this morning to my arm looking like this." She held out her arm.

"Ummm...it looks like a normal arm," Emma said. Was Isabelle hallucinating?

"Wait for it." She closed her eyes and the arm faded to a shadowy mist. She re-opened them and met Emma's gaze. "See?"

Emma gasped and put a hand to her mouth in shock. She'd seen that before. "You gained the same power your mother has?"

Isabelle closed her eyes once more and the arm re-materialized to flesh and bone. "I think so," she sounded more hesitant than Emma had ever heard her. "But I wasn't expecting it to happen. I thought it would not come, that I wouldn't have the power. My magic started when I was ten, so my mother told me she didn't think I would have her power if it didn't materialize at ten. My father disagreed, but I never thought he might be right..." she trailed off. "Emma, I'm scared."

"Scared of what?" Emma asked. "You're the bravest girl in this school and you have an *awesome* ability! I saw your mom transport an entire army from a battlefield to the Fields of Pelinor. This is going to be great."

"But I don't know how to use it," Isabelle said. "My mother never bothered to talk to me about how her ability worked because she didn't expect me to develop the power. I observed her shifting time and time again but she never took me into the shadow realm or explained how it felt to *be* a shifter. Do you get it now?" Isabelle sounded agitated, like she had expected a different reaction from Emma.

If we're truly friends then she deserves a different reaction. Emma sobered. She understood very well, now that Isabelle had laid her feelings bare. "Yes," she admitted, sighing as memories welled up inside her. "When my powers manifested I was scared too. My parents don't have magic, so they couldn't prepare me for what to expect. I'm sorry, I should have been more considerate."

Isabelle shook her head. "There's no need to apologize. But I'm glad you understand." She smiled shyly. "I am confident with my magic, and with weapons. My mother spent most of our time together teaching me how to fight, but shifting..." she paused, on the verge of repeating what she had already said.

"Do you want to go talk to Alivia?" Emma asked. "Maybe she could contact your mom and she could come teach you. Or at least show you the basics."

"I think that's a good idea. Will you come with me?"

"Of course!" Emma said. "I just hope we don't get scolded for being out past curfew...again."

Isabelle smiled. "Let's go." She rose and offered a hand to Emma.

Emma seized it and felt her stomach lurch. Her body was turning to shadowy mist. Some instinct deep inside her told her not to let go of Isabelle's hand if she wanted to live. Her eyes went wide with surprise, mirrored by Isabelle's own as her body too turned to mist. In moments the world around them faded to shadow, revealing a place Emma had stood in twice before - the shadow realm. "How?" was the only word that could escape her lips.

"I...I don't know," Isabelle sounded even more shaken than before. "But don't let go of my hand. Just in case."

"Can you get us back?"

"I'll try." She took a deep breath and closed her eyes. Emma felt a *tugging* but nothing happened. Isabelle's eyes snapped open. "It's not working." She started to breathe heavy, her eyes wide with panic.

Think, Emma, think. "Okay, it's okay. Calm down. Take deep breaths. Maybe you need to be calm to use your ability."

"I am calm!"

Emma snorted, unable to contain her laughter. "If that is you calm, I'd hate to see you panicked." She maintained her smile even as Isabelle shot her an angry glare.

"You're not helping." But then she broke into laughter. The two stood there laughing for half a minute or longer before they sobered up. "Thanks," she said, sounding much calmer.

"Any time," Emma said, meaning the words. This girl was just like her, not some royal brat in a palace or merchant's daughter used to having everything handed to her by her father. Yes, her parents were famous heroes, but Isabelle was not. It was easy to not be able to see her beneath the shadow of her parents. It was a problem Emma did not have, but now saw in the way she had treated Isabelle the last few days. *She just wanted to be treated normal.* "Do you want to try again?"

Isabelle nodded, closing her eyes again. Emma felt a chill run up her spine this time and their surroundings shifted. But they did not find themselves in the real world. Instead they found themselves somewhere else in the shadow realm.

The building they stood in bore no resemblance to the Tower. Or at least, no section of the Tower Emma remembered visiting or hearing about. A strange mechanism of orbs, with one orb the size of several carts side-by-side in the center and numerous smaller orbs of various sizes rotating around the central orb, hung beneath a high vaulted ceiling made entirely of glass. Though they were in the shadow realm, where colors were banished, Emma got the distinct impression of light flowing in through the ceiling and striking the orbs. The shafts of the light moved around the room, reflecting off the orbs. *They must be metal or glass orbs*, Emma guessed. "Where are we?" she asked, more in awe than in fright.

"I don't know," Isabelle said absently.

"What did you think about when you tried to shift us back?" Emma asked.

"I thought about returning to reality. I thought about light and color and...oh."

"What?"

"That mechanism. It's reflecting sunlight. I bet there is a prism somewhere up there which splits out the sunlight into different colors - like a rainbow."

Emma frowned. She had seen rainbows, but she didn't know what a prism was. She opened her mouth to ask, but then realized it didn't matter in the moment. "So can you envision the Tower and get us back?"

"I'm trying," her friend snapped. "Sorry." She hung her head as if in shame. "This is my first time doing this."

"It's okay. Just close your eyes and envision us back in the Tower. Or in the real world."

Isabelle closed her eyes again and this time Emma felt a tingling run across her skin. The gray receded in an instant, replaced by wondrous light. The prisms Isabelle had spoken of sent rainbow beams streaming in multiple directions, while reflected regular sunlight beamed straight down toward the center of the building, close to where Emma and Isabelle stood.

"Well, you brought us back to the real world," Emma said. "That's something."

"In an unknown place," Isabelle pointed out.

Emma shrugged. "Baby steps." She studied their surroundings and shivered. "It's chilly in here." It reminded her of Ironforge in the midst of winter. She walked toward the light at the center of the structure, hoping for warmth.

"Wait. Are you sure it's safe?"

Emma stopped short of the pillar of light and gingerly extended her hand. Nothing happened except gentle warmth enveloping her flesh, banishing the cold. She looked over her shoulder. "It's safe." She stepped forward and let the dense light wash over her and banish the chill air. They must have physically traveled if they were feeling cold of this magnitude.

Isabelle joined her in the light and let out a sigh of pleasure. "I'm not accustomed to the cold. My father's ships usually sail the warmer waters. We rarely venture north."

"Well I *am* used to it and it's still cold," Emma consoled her. "Any idea what this place could be?" *Or where?*

Isabelle shook her head. "No. Want me to try to shift us again?"

Though she was afraid of once again being stuck in the shadow realm, she was more afraid of being stranded in an unknown building. There weren't any signs of people, though there was also no sign of decay or dust. *Is it abandoned or inhabited?* She wondered. "Hello!" she shouted. Her voice echoed through the cavernous hall. Hallways at intervals along the wall led in different directions. The alternating rainbow patterns made it difficult for her to focus.

A focused beam of light shot out of one of the orbs and struck the ground. The light grew up from the ground and in seconds formed a person. The image of a man, perhaps in his forties, with black hair and wearing a fancy vest over a shirt and dress pants studied them. "Ah, visitors. Please state your names."

Emma blinked. Was that a real man or... "Are you real?"

"I assure you I am not a hallucination. Though I am not flesh and blood, I am a fully functional artificial intelligence program designed to assist in the operation of this facility."

Emma groaned. Another entity like Shadow. "What facility is this?"

He cocked his head to the side. "You entered and you do not know the designation of this facility?"

"We came here by accident," Isabelle interjected.

"Well, you are in the Halls of Light." He seemed to pause for dramatic effect.

Emma decided to disabuse him of the assumption that they knew what that meant. "What are the Halls of Light?"

"The Halls of Light are a repository for all human knowledge. They house samples of and data on the most advanced innovations known to man."

"Why have we never heard of them then?"

"I do not know. It has been," he paused, "twenty years since we last had a visitor. I am led to believe the identity of this facility has been kept a closely guarded secret."

Emma frowned. "Where are the Halls of Light located?"

A beam of light shot out of another orb and spread wide, forming into the shape of a glowing ball. Shapes formed on the ball, some green and others blue. Emma thought it looked like a map. "Is this a map of the world?" she asked.

"Correct. This is a representation of your world based upon the last survey. The Halls of Light are here." Though the map didn't grow larger, it did seem to change the image to focus on one particular area of the map, the White Mountains. Then it focused again, on a northern section of the White Mountains near Ironforge. It morphed again and the image of a towering central building with seven exterior buildings standing around it, connected with what looked like tubes, though Emma knew they were hallways, came into view. Their building.

"So we're in the mountains," Emma observed. And in the northern part of the mountain chain, to boot. That explained the cold. "You brought us to the mountains in the blink of an eye." That was hundreds of miles away from Tar Ebon. It had taken her mother a few jumps to take them from a location southwest of here but closer to Tar Ebon back to the Fields of Pelinor outside the city. Did that mean Isabelle was more powerful? Or just that it took less energy to transport two people than it did an entire army? She certainly didn't know enough about her friend's powers to make even a remotely accurate guess.

"Yeah," Isabelle said, sounding surprised.

"What is your name?" Emma asked the artificial man.

"I am called A.L., short for Artificial Librarian."

"So that's what you are? A librarian?"

"Yes. My primary function is to curate and organize the library and assist guests in finding particular records."

"Sounds fun," Isabelle said sarcastically.

The man tilted his head. "It is my job. I am programmed to find it compelling and do the best job possible."

"Do you know how we can get out of here?" Emma asked.

"The shadow gate is currently non-functional," Al explained. "How did you arrive here?" His voice did not convey puzzlement, simply a neutral question.

"We...uh...shifted," Emma said, looking at Isabelle. "Into the shadow realm, then returned to reality here."

"Ah, a warp anomaly."

Isabelle bristled, presumably at being called an anomaly. "Are you calling me strange?"

"No," Al said in a matter-of-fact tone. "I am defining the event that caused your re-emergence from the shadow realm. My sensors detected the anomaly as you warped, or shifted, as you call it, back to real-space."

"Oh," Isabelle said in a sheepish tone. "Sorry for snapping at you."

"You do not need to apologize to me. I am unable to take offense."

"While we're here," Emma began, curiosity getting the better of the fear she'd felt upon first arriving there. "Can you show us around?"

"But of course. I would be delighted to give you a personal tour." His voice became deeper. "However, I must verify that you are authorized first. Please stand still."

Before either girl could say a word, Al had activated multiple beams of light that shot out from miniature projectors which popped out of the walls and columns. The beams of light twisted and became flat, scanning each girl from top to bottom. The beams seemed to linger on their heads for a moment longer than the rest of their bodies. Moments later the beams blinked out of existence.

"Access to the minimum security section is granted," Al said, returning to his more conversational, friendly, tone. "Please follow me."

The girls shared a quick glance. "Do you want to follow him?" Isabelle asked.

Emma shrugged. "It won't hurt, will it? He said it houses advanced innovations. I'm curious, aren't you?"

Isabelle nodded, clearly seeing Emma's logic. "Yeah. Let's go."

The friends followed the projected image of Al as he led them toward one of the hallways leading away from the main chamber. Emma wondered how he would pass into the hallway if he was being projected from the orb in the central chamber, but her question was answered a moment later when projectors popped out of the walls of the hallway ahead of their advance and continued the illusion of Al. *This is a smart building*, she thought.

The building houses a powerful AI, Shadow interjected. I sense strong currents of electricity and magnetism throughout the walls of this place.

Oh, now you join us. Did you sense when Al scanned us?

Of course. I am always active.

But you didn't say anything.

There was nothing to notify you about.

What was the scan looking for?

It appeared to be scanning your blood. It also pinged my communication array.

It must have been the blood that let us proceed, Emma posited. Maybe it sensed the magic in our blood. Because Isabelle doesn't have an implant like I do.

Shadow did not reply. It irritated her how he would fall silent in the midst of a conversation sometimes, but then she had told him to keep quiet several times. Still, there did not seem to be a logic behind when he chose to speak. And her thoughts about his illogical logic did not prompt him to respond, though she was sure he could hear or detect her thoughts.

They traveled down the hallway and emerged in a smaller circular building that resembled the main building almost exactly, down to the glass ceiling and orb mechanism high above, only on a smaller scale.

Emma gaped at the contents. Bookshelves lined all four walls and rows of bookshelves filled the center. Down one of the aisles she could see what looked like tables in the distance.

Al continued forward, the light from the hallway fading and the orb granting him his substance now. "This is the historical section. It contains ancient records from Earth prior to the Founding."

"What is Earth?" Emma asked.

"Where the Founders came from," Al said, as if it should be obvious.

"Is that another continent?" She knew about the storm wall to the south. Could it have been a land beyond the storm wall and the Founders sailed north to found Tar Ebon?

"No. It is another planet. Would you like more information?"

Emma stood glued to her spot, too shocked to speak. "Another planet?" she repeated. She knew the stars in the sky were suns - her father had told her that. And she knew planets orbited those distant suns. But...she had never thought people might *live* on those other planets. "Did you know about this?" she asked Isabelle.

Isabelle's wide eyes answered her question. She had no idea. She shook her head as confirmation. "My parents never mentioned anything like that."

Al began to speak, evidently taking Emma's question as an invitation to provide more information. "The planet Earth was the home of the Founders." Another image appeared above him, floating several feet off the ground. It took on blues and greens with hints of tan and brown, building layer-upon-layer until what looked like a miniature model of a planet floated there. It floated down to hover only a foot or two off the ground, allowing the girls to approach. "In the twenty-fourth century AD the Earth Federation had colonized dozens of planets and built a strong inter-stellar coalition of planets." An image of metal ships floating in the dark of space above Earth appeared.

"But it was not to be." New ships appeared, strange green and brown-looking ships in oblong shapes with bumpy surfaces. They fired green rocks toward the metal ships, which in turn caused them to explode and shatter into thousands of illuminated pieces. "The Krai'kesh discovered the Earth Federation and attacked them. War raged for many years, with the Earth Federation consistently losing ground. Eventually, a brilliant scientist discovered a way to send ships and people back in time. Tar Ebon was chosen, based upon archaeological evidence suggesting Tar Ebon had developed faster than Earth but had been cut short in its development due to a Krai'kesh incursion. As Earth, and the rest of the Federation, fell, the eight arc ships were sent through time and space. Seven arrived on Tar Ebon, while the eighth was lost. So the Founders came to Tar Ebon." The image of destruction was placed with an image of a new planet, different from Earth yet similar in that it too was composed of blues and greens and browns.

"Did they all land in the same place?"

"Several of the arc ships sustained damage from the trip and entered Tar Ebon's orbit at rapid rates and without navigational assistance or maneuvering capabilities. They crash-landed at various points across the world." Lights blinked on the image of Tar Ebon floating before them. Seven images in all, she discovered, as the globe spun. Four in the northern hemisphere, including Shar'hai and Tar Ebon and two on the side the Rakosh Empire dominated. Three blinked in the southern hemisphere, below the representation of the storm wall, which spanned the globe. There in the south, two cities sat upon one large continent while another, smaller continent, sat across the ocean from that continent. "Are there any further questions?"

Emma's head spun from the depth of knowledge imparted by Al. To think their ancestors came from the stars, from another place in time, shocked her to her core. "Were there people on this planet before the Founders came?" She suspected she knew the answer but felt compelled to ask.

"There were many indigenous civilizations and peoples inhabiting the planet when the Founders came. Some welcomed them, while others fought them and still others assimilated with their culture. The numeral system and common tongue are remnants from the Founders."

"Why is this stuff locked away atop a mountain?" Isabelle asked. "My father would love this place."

"The Halls of Light were created by the Founders as a repository for all human knowledge. However, the knowledge was deemed too dangerous to be disseminated at the time. The Halls were locked until the appropriate time."

"I guess this is the appropriate time," Emma said. "Is every room filled with books?"

"Four of the seven halls are indeed libraries. They specialize in different levels of knowledge, based upon complexity and danger level. The remaining levels contain functional prototypes of select technologies. However, these, along with two of the library halls, are locked based upon your current permission level."

I wonder what it would take to get full permission, Emma wondered. "We should probably get back," she said, shivering again. "It's cold in here and the school will miss us."

"We can modulate the temperature in here to a more comfortable level," Al said. Immediately, heat began to radiate from the walls, floors and ceilings. "But, I understand. Please follow me back to the main hall." Al led them back the way they'd come to the central building. "Thank you for visiting the Halls of Light. I do hope you enjoyed your visit." His image faded and he was gone.

Emma looked at Isabelle. "Do you think you can get us out of here now?"

"Do I have a choice?" The other girl shrugged. She answered her own question a moment later. "Not if I don't want us to die here."

A thought struck Emma just then. "I might be able to send a message to Tar Ebon."

"How?" Isabelle asked.

Emma hesitated. She trusted Isabelle, but what she would tell her would probably come as a shock. She took a deep breath. "When my brother and I used the Staff of Agamar *something* happened and we unlocked something inside us."

"Like stronger magic or something?"

"No, sort of like a voice in our heads. They are implants housing artificial intelligences." That last sentence sounded foreign to her. She still didn't fully understand what they meant.

"Oh, like my mom and dad," her friend replied. "So you and Ethan can communicate over long distance?"

"We *might* be able to," Emma said. "We were able to in Tar Ebon but...I don't know the limitations."

"Worth a shot. Though I'm not sure what he'll be able to do to help us."

"He could tell Alivia or get a message to your mother. Then maybe she could come and rescue us?"

Isabelle nodded. "Yeah, that could work. Try it."

Emma closed her eyes. *Shadow?*

Yes?

You must have heard that conversation. Can you connect with Ethan?

I was but waiting for you to make the request, m'lady. One moment while I attempt to establish a connection. The link went silent as Emma got the sense Shadow was no longer listening to her before he returned. I have established a connection. You may speak to him, though the reception in this region is spotty. You may not be able to speak to one another for long.

Okay, thanks. She still marveled at the capability for long-distance communication, no matter how long it lasted. She sensed her brother in the back of her mind and focused on him. *Ethan?*

Hey sis, what's up?

Emma swallowed, her mouth suddenly dry. Why was she nervous about this? Was she worried she would be disciplined again for disappearing accidentally from the Tower? *Listen. I need you to find Alivia right away. You need to tell her that Isabelle and I accidentally ended up at the Halls of Light. She needs to get in touch with Bridgette and send help. Got all that?*

The link was silent for so long that Emma wondered if her twin were still on the other end. *Are you there?*

That's so cool! He shouted through the link, causing Emma's head to whip back as if he'd been yelling in her ear.

So you'll do it? Emma pressed.

Yeah, of course. Might take me a bit to find her, though. What are the Halls of Light?

I'll explain later. Just go, please?

Okay. Want to stay on the line with me while I look?

No. Just try to link up with me when you've reached her and have something to report. Deal?

Deal. Talk to you soon. The link faded, although her brother's presence was once again lodged in the back of her mind, as it had been back at Tar Ebon. The shock of arriving in a new place had overshadowed the loss of his presence and Emma hadn't noticed its absence until it returned.

"He's going to try his best," she explained to Isabelle.

She nodded. "Do you want to go back and keep exploring? Or should I keep trying to shift?"

The idea of a treasure trove of scarce-known or long-forgotten knowledge tantalized Emma. She longed to return to the library and begin reading book after book. But she hesitated. Kyra was still in the Tower, causing the Founders knew what trouble, planning who knew what. Plus there was their training to consider. She couldn't just abandon her training. *We could just go exploring while waiting for Ethan to report back, right? Surely that wouldn't hurt.*

"Try to shift, I guess."

Isabelle closed her eyes and her legs began to turn to black mist.

"Uh, Isabelle..." Emma began.

Isabelle's eyes snapped open and her legs returned to solid form. "What?"

"Your legs were turning to mist. That's good, right?"

"I think so. Take my hand, in case it works this time. I should have thought of that sooner."

Yes, I would hate being stranded here alone, with only two artificial men to talk to.

I heard that, Shadow chimed in. I will have you know that I am a much better conversationalist than the AI you call Al.

Is somebody jealous?

No, of course not.

Emma snorted but let the matter drop as she took Isabelle's hand.

Isabelle closed her eyes and this time Emma felt the sensation of her legs and then lower body fading moments later. Within a few seconds they had entered the shadow realm completely.

Chapter 12

The Halls of Light inside the shadow realm looked like it had before they arrived. "Let's walk around in here," Isabelle suggested. Still holding hands, the girls walked down one of the other hallways and entered a room filled with more books and laid out in a similar manner to the first room Al had shown them. The next two rooms were the same style, but the fourth room they visited held strange devices that boggled Emma's mind, even if they weren't in gray scale. There were items with long, hollow cylinders on one end and what looked like triangle at the other end and a curved piece of metal in front of the triangle. Emma looked at Isabelle quizzically. "I think it's a gun," she said, the word sounding foreign even to her. "My father is experimenting with something called gunpowder and muskets, a type of gun, aboard our ship."

"Do they look anything like this?" Emma reached out to touch the gun but her hand passed right through as if she were made of vapor. Of course people in the shadow realm would not be able to touch the physical realm. They were merely a reflection of themselves.

"The basic design is similar. But the barrel, that long hollow part, is longer and it has a hammer at the back of it and a piece of rope that you're supposed to light on fire to ignite the gunpowder. My father says it propels a projectile, like a rock, only smoother, toward a target. I lost interest when he started babbling about rifling and clips and more."

"Oh. It sounds like your father babbles a lot," Emma observed.

Isabelle snorted but avoided Emma's gaze. "You don't know the half of it. He spends most of his days locked in his lab. I was surprised he even accompanied Mother to help you. I think he only went because of some Staff."

"The Staff of Agamar," Emma explained. "It was a powerful artifact." *It nearly killed me.*

"Yeah. And you can bet if my father could get up here he would be playing with all these artifacts," she cast an arm out to encompass the room full of strange technologies.

Emma tried to comprehend the other items in the room. One artifact looked like panels of glass leaned against the wall with shelves jutting out below them. As she and Isabelle approached, she saw raised pieces of a strange material marked with symbols. Letters and numbers, she realized after a moment. "Any idea what this is?" she asked.

Isabelle shook her head. "None. Okay let's...," she let go of Emma's hand and clutched her head with her hands and let out a scream.

"Isabelle!" Emma said, trying to look into her eyes. "What's wrong?"

"My head. I feel...something," the act of speaking seemed to be taking its toll on her. "Something...beckoning..." she pointed toward the opposite wall. "From the east." She screamed again, louder. "Have to...go..."

On instinct, Emma grabbed Isabelle's hand. Not a moment too soon, either, for an instant later the landscape shifted and they were in the woods. Massive trees that would dwarf those around Ironforge rose high above. *The Gallean forests?* She wondered. Isabelle grunted, still clutching her head. Blink. The landscape shifted again, this time to the shoreline. Waves crashed against the beach. An island sat in the distance, with a dark cloud hovering above it. *I have a bad feeling about this.* Blink. They stood at the edge of the swirling darkness. Isabelle fell to her knees and breathed a sigh of relief.

"What happened?" Emma asked. "Where are we?"

An evil laugh echoed from within the fog concealing their sight. The source of the laugh appeared a moment later, striding out of the darkness. He wore black armor and a helmet with horns sticking straight up. In one hand he held a wicked-looking scepter, in the other a spiked shield. "You have arrived at my prison," the figure said. "Long have I waited for you, child of shadow."

He had to be speaking of Isabelle. Emma, still keeping a grip on her friend's hand, stepped between them. "Stay away from her." She tried to summon her magic, but it felt far away, as if it were across a vast canyon.

The man was silent for a moment, as if assessing Emma. "Like a parasite clinging to its host. But I smell magic on you." He tilted his head. "Yes. Great power lives within you. Who are your parents?"

"Nobodies," she answered truthfully. "But my name is Emma, and you will have to go through me to get to her."

"Ah, such nobility." He flicked his hand and Emma's grip on Isabelle's hand broke. He stretched out his hand, holding it like a C. She flew straight toward him and a moment later his gauntleted fist clutched her throat. She groped desperately for her magic while her fingers clawed at the metal. She couldn't breathe. Panic assailed her mind. *Must do something. Must escape. I can't let this be the end.* Her thoughts became sluggish as his grip tightened. "I could crush you like a gnat."

Warning, oxygen levels dangerously low. Activating emergency oxygenation protocol. Emma felt the panic subside, at least a little, as whatever Shadow had done took effect and the cloud on her mind lifted, if temporarily. She had to use the additional time to her advantage. Again she reached for her magic but felt it at a distance still. *How do I close the gap?* Her magic was the manipulation of the physical realm, so it made sense it couldn't affect the shadow realm. But what if...

Her thoughts were cut off as Isabelle shouted, "Let her go!" Emma couldn't see her face, couldn't move, but she imagined her friend with a fierce look on her face.

"Now you show a backbone, girl. I will spare your friend *if* you swear fealty to me. Bend the knee and swear yourself my servant and I will let dear Emma live."

"No," Emma croaked before the man tightened his grip, cutting off her words. *Don't do it*, she finished in her mind, though Isabelle could not hear her.

"I...swear..."

"Enough of this, Valdorf," a different female voice came from behind. Emma recognized that voice, even though the fog was returning in her mind. *Bridgette*.

The man, Valdorf, released Emma, shoving her dozens of feet to land on the beach. She did not taste sand in her mouth, for the sand didn't exist here. How she stood upon it was a mystery to her. It was as if the physical world affected the shadow realm but not to the full extent. There *had* to be a way for her to use her magic here. She came to her feet and looked toward Bridgette.

Isabelle's mother stood next to her daughter. She wore a cloak with the hood down and carried a pair of short swords in her hands. Her expressionless face turned toward Emma. She met her eyes and gave a brief nod of her head before returning her gaze to Valdorf. "This is *my* domain. How dare you try to bring my daughter into this?"

"Ah, the mama bear arrives to protect her cub. You overestimate your power in this realm." He gestured behind himself. "My power grows. Your prison will not hold me for long."

"Then maybe I should gut you where you stand and end this," Bridgette replied.

The man threw back his head and laughed. "You would have killed me twenty years ago if you could have. You and I both know I am immortal."

The look on Bridgette's face told Emma that Valdorf spoke the truth. "That may be true...for now...but I can still throw you back into your prison and throw away the key."

"A temporary action by a scared assassin," Valdorf mocked. "It is only a matter of time and I shall return to your world stronger than ever." He brandished his mace. "Come and fight me. Let me taste blood on my lips once more." He licked his mace.

"You're not worth my time," Bridgette countered. She sent a ball of pure shadow toward the man, which sent him flying backward into the cloud of darkness he'd walked out of. She then grabbed Isabelle's arm and the two of them disappeared, only to reappear a moment later beside Emma. Her hand wrapped around Emma's arm and the landscape changed, though Valdorf's maniacal laughter echoed after them. They found themselves once again in the shadowy representation of the Halls of Light. In a flash they re-entered the physical realm.

Emma blanched and stumbled away from the others. The gravity of what had just happened crashed into her mind. She had almost died. She put a hand to her throat, still feeling Valdorf's evil presence and his gauntleted hand. "Who..." *Come on, pull yourself together.* She began again. "Who was he?"

Bridgette eyed her, sympathy on her face. "That was Valdorf, an evil sorcerer."

"How did he get into the shadow realm?" Emma pressed. "He said something about being imprisoned there?"

Bridgette nodded. "Twenty years ago he was imprisoned in the shadow realm. I was the one who imprisoned him there, after a long fight in which your...the other Eternals and I defeated him."

"Why didn't you just kill him?" Isabelle asked, echoing the question swirling around in Emma's mind.

"We couldn't. He was protected by powerful enchantments that did not permit him to die. Not permanently. This was a...temporary solution, until your father could figure out something better."

"And has Father figured out something more permanent?" Isabelle asked.

"Not yet. But now that we are in the Halls of Light...that could change."

"Wait. You were never here before?" Emma asked.

"No. We didn't know the location of this place until word came through Alivia that you and Isabelle were trapped here. I tracked her signature and came here. Then, not finding you here, I followed you to Valdorf's prison."

Indeed, Al stood by, silent but watching the exchange. When Emma looked at him, he smiled and spoke. "Mistress Emma, it is good to see you back so soon."

"I wish it were under better circumstances," Emma replied, rubbing at her throat again. "Where is your husband?"

"Down that way," Bridgette pointed toward a room Emma had seen whilst in the shadow realm. That was the room with the models of advanced technology, wasn't it?

"He was allowed in there?" Emma asked. "Al said we had limited permissions."

"Yes. We were granted full access due to our...unique nature."

Emma didn't doubt her words, and she doubted Al would have been standing there smiling calmly if Bridgette and Jason had entered without permission. "Oh," was all she said.

"Can I go see him?" Isabelle asked.

"I don't see why not," Bridgette replied. She looked at the image of Al. "What say you, Al? Will you grant these girls full permissions?"

"With your authorization I can pass down permissions," Al began, "to her," he pointed to Emma. "She will need to activate her implant before full access can be granted." This time his finger pointed to Isabelle.

"Implant?" Isabelle asked, brow furrowing. "What implant is he talking about?"

Bridgette sighed. "I suppose this conversation was overdue." She looked her daughter in the eyes. "It's time for a talk."

"Mom, we already had the talk," Isabelle said tensely.

"This is more...intricate than the maturity talk." She folded her hands and took a deep breath before speaking. "You were born with an artificial intelligence embedded in your mind. It exists in the form of a chip that resides in your skull." She tapped her own head. "Your father and I both have one, and the nanites in our blood, and thus in yours upon conception..."

"Mom!"

"...created the implant shortly after your birth. However, the implant was programmed to remain dormant until specific criteria were met."

"Such as?"

Isabelle's mother ticked up a finger. "One, if your life were threatened, the implant would activate, regardless of age or maturity."

That is what happened with me, Emma thought. Isn't it?

She ticked up a second finger. "Two, when you reached the age of eighteen it would activate by default."

"Happy birthday to me," Isabelle grumbled. "So it's still dormant until I turn eighteen? Or do you have to stab me?"

Bridgette smiled slightly. "Violence will not be necessary. There is a failsafe, which can activate the implant despite the first two criterion not being met. Your father will need to activate it, however. Al, can you allow temporary access to Isabelle?"

"While in your presence she will be permitted," Al responded. "But please be warned that any unauthorized departure from your presence while in a restricted area will be met with deadly force."

"Ironic," Bridgette said. "Come along." She beckoned for the girls to follow her.

"Wait," Isabelle said. "How did you get an implant in your head, Emma?"

Emma shrugged. Isabelle knew about her implant - she'd told her about it when she contacted Ethan to seek out Alivia and ask for help. "I don't know. I'm not special like you. My parents are normal. I think it might have been the Staff of Agamar that implanted Ethan and I, since it was both of us who touched it."

Isabelle nodded slowly. "That makes some sense."

The girls walked in silence down the hall as they followed Isabelle's mother. They reached the room they'd visited only in the shadow realm and found Jason hunched over in front of one of the massive glass screens. Except now the glass screen was not blank - images and symbols flashed across the huge screen, apparently changing in response to the tapping of buttons by Jason's hands.

"Jason," Bridgette said. "Your daughter is back, safe and sound."

Jason grunted but did not look up. "So the quantum co-efficient of the inverse..." he muttered to himself.

"Excuse my husband," Bridgette said to Emma. "In this place he is like a kid in the candy store."

"This technology will revolutionize the world," Jason said. "This was the missing link. No more having to go off memory or vague records. There are schematics and drawings and illustrations and simulations and..." he finally stood straight and spun around. "It's beyond our wildest dreams. It's like finding El Dorado, Bridgette."

The reference was lost on Emma, but she got the gist and assumed that was a good thing.

"Hi, Dad," Isabelle said, smiling nervously.

"Hey, Pumpkin," Jason said, finally seeming to notice his daughter. He flung his arms out wide, silently requesting a hug.

Isabelle went and flung herself into his arms, then nestled her head against his chest. Emma half-expected there to be tears, after all the girl had just gone through, but none came. *Of course not. She's the daughter of an assassin. She wouldn't cry easily...if at all.*

The two broke apart moments later and Jason looked to his wife. "So Valdorf is truly free?"

Bridgette shook her head. "Not quite. He can leave his prison but only a short radius around it, from what I could see. He's dangerous, and we need to find a solution to end him permanently, but for now he's contained." The *for now* seemed to hang in the air. She cleared her throat. "But there is another matter that brought us in here," she went on, "Isabelle needs access to her implant."

Jason blinked. "Oh. You...told her about that, did you?" He offered a wan smile. "You seemed to take it well."

Isabelle punched her dad in the gut. "I'm furious that you guys kept it a secret from me for so long." But then she smiled. "But it does sound pretty cool, so I'll forgive you."

"Two abilities in one day," her father muttered. "Shadow walking and an implant activation. Are you sure she's ready for this?"

"She can never be fully ready," Bridgette said. "I will have to work on her shifting with her, but her implant will be of great advantage to her, both with her shifting and at the Tower."

"Yes, yes, implants can help with navigational capabilities," Jason muttered, almost to himself again. "Okay, so you want me to activate the failsafe?"

"Preferably," Bridgette said dryly. "Otherwise it require a time machine or stabbing."

"Eh, a time machine wouldn't work," Jason said. "It wouldn't change her biological age."

"I was joking, dear."

"Oh, right." He chuckled, then placed his hands on either side of Isabelle's head. "This shouldn't hurt. Just close your eyes." He closed his own eyes too.

For a long moment, nothing happened. Emma resisted the urge to look around the intriguing room out of boredom as she waited for whatever Jason was doing to take effect. Then Isabelle gasped, eyes going wide. "Wow," was all she said.

Wow was right. Emma recalled the feeling of surprise and wonder when Shadow had first activated. Granted, she hadn't been expecting the presence of an artificial intelligence in her head, while Isabelle was. But still, the presence of wonder would still be there. She couldn't help smiling at her friend's pleasure.

"I can feel...everything. My whole body," she said. "And this place, I can see it in my mind."

Emma frowned. *How come I can't do that*? She wondered.

You can, Shadow informed her dryly. *You have but to ask.*

Well, you could have given me a tour or something.

Would you like a tour right now?

No. No time right now. Maybe when we're back safe at the Tower.

I shall add it to your schedule.

You can schedule things for me?

Of course. Though my capabilities are wasted acting as only a personal assistant.

I'll keep that in mind, Emma thought dryly.

"An implant can be quite useful," Isabelle's father said. "Most importantly due to the control they exert over the nanites in your blood. Without your implant, the nanites would be non-functional."

"What do the nanites do?" Isabelle asked. "Wait. Valerie answered me."

Who is Valerie? Emma wondered. Then answered herself. *Oh, her implant.*

Her parents must have understood as well, for they both nodded. "I'm sure you're implant answered you in-detail," Jason said. "But in short, nanites primarily serve as a healing agent in your body. They can cluster together to quickly heal wounds or purge poison from your body. The mere presence of an active implant can also protect against compulsion spells."

"Which is another reason I wanted her implant activated," Bridgette explained. "It sounds like Valdorf compelled you to come to him, is that correct Isabelle?"

Isabelle nodded. "I felt this...tug...on me and felt like I had to go in that direction while I was in the shadow realm. I didn't know what was going on."

And I was along for the ride, Emma thought ruefully.

"It was my fault for not preparing you for the shadow realm," her mother said. "I honestly didn't expect you to develop the power after puberty came and went and only your magic developed."

"I told you we didn't know enough about how shifting powers worked," Jason admonished, the first time Emma had heard him scolding his wife. "I was right."

Bridgette raised an eyebrow at her husband. "Go ahead, gloat some more. Gloat and get back to your computer."

"It's a quantum computer," Jason corrected.

"Same difference. I'm going to take these two back to the Tower. Will you survive here until I get back?"

Jason was already walking toward the "computer," as he'd called it. He waved a hand over his shoulder as if to say goodbye. "Yeah, yeah, I'll be fine. Go ahead. I have Al to keep me company."

"Just don't forget to eat," Bridgette said, but Jason didn't answer. She sighed. "Both of you take a hand." She held her arms out to the side.

Emma took one hand, while Isabelle took the other. In a flash the light, and Jason, faded and the gray of the shadow realm embraced them once more.

Chapter 13

It took Bridgette two hops to bring them to Tar Ebon. They arrived in the courtyard. "Wait here," Bridgette instructed.

Emma remained where she was, looking up at the sun. Only a few hours had passed, by the looks of it. It had seemed much, much longer.

Alivia emerged from the Tower a minute later and ran to them. "What happened?" she demanded as she embraced the two girls. Her question seemed directed at Bridgette. But the assassin looked instead to Emma.

Emma braced herself for the torrent of questions she knew would come. "It's a long story. Can we talk in your office?"

For a moment Emma worried Alivia would demand they spill the beans right then and there. But if they did that, the gossips would have hold of it in minutes and the rest of the Tower would soon know what had happened. The arch mage seemed to realize that, for she gestured for the girls to follow her up the ramp into the tower. When Emma looked back to say goodbye to Bridgette, she found the woman gone. "Does she always do that?"

"Disappear without a word?" Isabelle asked sarcastically. "Yes." The second sentence sounded worn down and tired.

They made their way into the Tower and the elevator, then rode it up to the arch mage's office. Inside, they found Ethan with his feet up on the desk. A stern-sounding throat clearing from Alivia caused him to hastily remove them.

"Now, who wants to begin telling me what happened?" Alivia asked.

Emma and Isabelle shared a glance, each girl thinking about who wanted to go first. Emma raised her hand after the silence stretched several seconds too long. "I will."

Alivia nodded, encouraging her to go on.

Emma recounted the tale. Everything from Isabelle waking her up to appearing at the Halls of Light and then going back to the shadow realm after calling for help and seeing Valdorf. She noticed Alivia's face seemed to pale upon hearing the news they'd seen the evil sorcerer and brightened upon hearing of the Halls of Light.

"We thought the Halls of Light a myth, legend, or misinterpretation of the ancient texts," Alivia said when Emma finished. "I am surprised the two of you found it by accident. But by the sounds of it, if Jason is there investigating it was a good thing you did."

Emma nodded. "And Valdorf?"

"As Bridgette told you, we fought and defeated him twenty years ago. If he has returned..." she fell silent, staring blankly past the three students, "we will need to muster the forces to defeat him a second time. Though I fear it will not be as easy, for the cult that follows him is stronger this time around."

"The Cult of Rae?" Emma guessed.

"Yes. They follow the god of the Krai'kesh in principle, but in reality, their leader is Valdorf. He claims to interpret the will of Rae'Shela on this world. He's clearly insane, but those seeking to destroy the world will gravitate to the most powerful people they can find."

Ethan raised a hand, then spoke without waiting for acknowledgment. "Quick question. Did you bring back any souvenirs?"

Emma fought down the urge to slap her brother. "No. We were a little preoccupied to concern ourselves with souvenirs. Besides, I don't think the artificial intelligence defending the Halls of Light wouldn't have liked that."

Ethan shrugged. "Eh, it was worth asking."

Alivia rolled her eyes but did not admonish Ethan for asking what she most likely thought was also a stupid question. "I am glad the two of you are safe. Now return to your rooms and clean yourselves up, then resume your studies. If Valdorf is nearing freedom it is all the more important that we have as many trained mages ready to face him and his minions as possible."

Emma nodded. That made sense, though the three of them were only first year students. Unless Valdorf came several years later, they likely wouldn't be of much use against him. Still, some training was better than no training, wasn't it?

"You are dismissed."

The trio rose and walked to the elevator, then went down to their floor. Emma went inside and found the common room a bustle of activity as morning came to the Tower. She realized she and Isabelle had gone further east, where the sun had risen earlier, and since it had only been an hour or two the sun was still only barely risen there at the Tower. She received a nod from her roommate Agnes and a scowl from Kyra.

The prefect stormed up to her and pointed a finger at Emma's chest. "Where were you?"

"I don't know what you mean?" Emma asked, trying to sound as innocent as possible.

"Don't play coy with me. You weren't in your rooms this morning. Where did you go?"

Isabelle didn't hang around to answer. She brushed by Kyra, almost contacting her shoulder, before going to her room.

"None of your business," Emma said bluntly, knowing that someone had to answer the girl. "If you want to report us, fine. But Arch Mage O'Leary knows where we were and approved of us being there." *Okay, so that's a lie. She approved of us being there after the fact.* Still, it truly was not any of Kyra's business.

Kyra sniffed. "I'll be watching you."

Likewise, Emma thought in return, though she said nothing. She maintained eye contact with the girl until the latter dropped her gaze and turned away. Then she made her way to her room. None of her roommates were present, which Emma preferred, under the circumstances. She quickly dressed for class and made her way back out into the common room. Kyra was nowhere to be seen, now. So Emma settled down to wait for Isabelle. As she sat, she let the recent experience wash over her. Disappearing, finding a place long hidden and then almost dying, a lot had happened in the space of a few hours.

Isabelle exited her room minutes later and they departed for class.

Chapter 14

The next three months settled into a dull routine of classwork, studying, sleeping and repeating. Fall had turned to winter and the first snow of the season had come to Tar Ebon. Emma watched with amusement as Isabelle marveled at the snow on the streets of Tar Ebon. The girl had spent most of her life aboard a ship in warmer waters, so it came as no surprise.

A cold wave washed over her body as a snowball hit the back of her neck. She spun around to see her brother rolling up yet another ball, Richard and Cadmon at his side. Even as she watched, Richard released a snowball and struck Kylie in the back. She too turned and glared at the boy.

Isabelle continued walking, holding out a gloved hand to study the snow. A snowball thrown by Cadmon arced through the air, aiming for the back of her neck, but her torso, neck, and head turned to shadow and it passed harmlessly through. She didn't even turn around, but a triumphant smirk appeared on her face. She had been practicing her shifting power for months with the aid of her mother, making for long days on top of her regular studies, but the results spoke for themselves.

"Awe," Cadmon said from behind. "That's cheating."

"You're lucky I just dodged your snowball. I could appear behind you and dump snow on your head before you could wonder where I went," Isabelle called over her shoulder.

"Will you go to the winter dance with me?" Cadmon called.

"Me?" Isabelle asked, sounding surprised.

"Of course."

This time Isabelle stopped, spinning around. "I don't dance," she said, as if he had asked if she would like to kiss a toad.

"I can teach you," Cadmon said, shrugging beneath the gaze of now three girls.

"Ignore him," Ethan said. "But you gotta give him credit for asking."

"Perhaps the professors will give me credit for asking if I can skip exams," Isabelle countered before turning around.

Emma smirked at her brother's gaping mouth and followed her friend. She felt confident calling Isabelle her friend now. Between class, sleep, studies and Isabelle's training they had spent much time getting to know one another. Emma felt a twinge of guilt while remembering. Kylie was still her friend, but they saw each other less. Being in different Houses meant they had different schedules and it was harder for them to sit up until the late hours of the night talking like she and Isabelle did. Still, she had been relieved when Kylie agreed to accompany them out on their first outing of the year.

"I need to find a dress for the dance," Emma said to her friends.

"Of course you would be going," Isabelle said. "Traitor." The words held no malice.

Emma resisted the urge to stick her tongue out, settling instead for a wide smile and elbowing Kylie. "What color dress are you looking for?" They were on their way to the tailor shop as she spoke.

"Hmmm?" Kylie asked, meeting Emma's eyes. "Oh, dresses. Ummm...green?"

"I'm looking for blue," Emma said, not commenting on Kylie's distractedness. The girl barely seemed there. Had she really wanted to come out with them or had she agreed out of politeness? Emma felt a gulf growing between them. A gulf she had to cross before it was too late. "How have your classes been going?" she pressed.

Kylie shrugged. "I'm doing well at the magic classes. It's the mundane courses that give me problems."

Emma nodded in sympathy. Aside from physical education, where Emma had done fairly well and even put on some muscle, and world history, which fascinated her, the other non-magical classes challenged her. It was easy to summon a fireball or throw up a shield or dissolve said fireball but understanding how different chemical ingredients combined or how advanced levels of mathematics worked was like trying to learn a whole different language. And her language arts class felt pointless. Yes, it was important to write clearly so that she could be understood. But was it necessary to read old stuffy stories and poems from now-dead authors and analyze them or define how those stories or poems made her "feel?" Emma didn't think so. "I know your pain."

"Why do they even make us take them?" Kylie went on. "We're here to become mages. Who cares if we can measure a triangle or know how to write a poem?"

Emma decided to recite the answer Alivia had given them. "Learning about these mundane topics helps us to become well-rounded mages capable of not just using magic but being a benefit to society."

"Well, I think that's rubbish."

"I don't know," Isabelle said. "My dad is a merchant as well as an inventor and he uses math all the time. Not to mention when he's designing a new ship. And my mother always stressed the importance of knowing the history of each culture we went to. It helped us fit in for the days or weeks we spent in their ports."

"You are the last person I would expect to defend boring classes at school," Kylie observed. "You seem like you hate school."

Isabelle shrugged. "What can I say? Maybe I'm a geek at heart."

"What's a geek?" Emma asked.

"Somebody who likes intellectual topics that others find strange," Isabelle said. "I'm paraphrasing. Basically like my father."

I certainly hope you don't become like your father, Emma thought. She couldn't see Isabelle stuck standing behind a work bench building new things and secluding herself from the world. The girl had too much of her mother in her for that.

The boys split off from the group when they arrived at the tailor. Emma asked if they were going to wear suits but the trio just laughed and headed toward the harbor. *Boys*, Emma thought.

The girls had spent an hour or more in the tailor's shop when the door opened and Kyra walked in with two of her friends. Emma glared at her. "What's *she* doing here?" she whispered to Isabelle, who followed her gaze. Intellectually Emma knew that if Kyra was also going to the dance she too would need a dress. But she suppressed that part of her brain.

"Probably here to cause trouble," Isabelle said, adding her glare to Emma's.

For Kyra's part, she cast a haughty glance in their direction and then seemed to stick her nose in the air and ignore them. She was going to treat them as if they didn't exist.

That response made Emma angrier than if the girl had glared back at them or said something to them. She formed her hands into fists and clenched her teeth. "Are you almost done?" she snapped as Kylie came out of the changing room.

Her friend started at the tone in her voice, looking at Emma askance before cautiously answering, "Yes, I liked this dress," she smoothed the long green dress that covered her from chin to toes. "Why? What's wrong?"

Emma shook her head, chastising herself mentally for snapping like that. "Kyra is here." She didn't bother to point the brat out. *Brat and maybe a traitor.* She hadn't forgotten what she'd heard. Was Kyra a traitor to the Tower?

"Oh," Kylie said. She didn't seem to possess the same level of hatred Isabelle and Emma did for the prefect of House Longclaw. But then, why would she? She was in a completely different house and would have rarely interacted with Kyra, if ever. And there was nothing in the unofficial rules of friendship forcing her to hate everyone who Emma or Isabelle hated.

"I'm going to step outside. Get some air." She said her last sentence louder on purpose, hoping Kyra would catch it. She stalked out of the store with her blue dress draped over her arm, Isabelle in tow. They stood outside watching as snow continued to fall while Kylie settled her account. While most students paid tuition to enter the Tower and were also given spending money by their families, the Tower did give scholarships to poorer students to ensure that anyone who wanted to learn could. Kylie had been the recipient of such a scholarship. Emma wasn't sure of the cost for her and Ethan's tuition, as her parents hadn't discussed the matter with her. They'd told her it wasn't important and that they had handled it.

The snow had continued its relentless fall from heaven while they were in the store. The streets had cleared slightly, with outdoor vendors packing up and townsfolk seeking shelter indoors. Tar Ebon was no stranger to snow, but Emma knew their winter season was far shorter than northern cities like Ironforge or the Haguesfort. Back home her parents would have had first snow two months ago and they would be buried under several feet of snow by now.

Emma tried to casually look inside the store, ostensibly to see what progress Kylie was making, but found herself glaring at Kyra. The two girls who had entered with her surrounded Kyra like servants, seeming to obey her every whim. Meanwhile, the owner of the shop had materialized to assist while Kylie was left in the care of the assistant. *She's being treated like royalty.* Kyra glanced toward the window and smirked at Emma, as if she had known she was watching the entire time. Emma averted her gaze and looked to Isabelle, who hadn't been watching Kyra. "So, how are you finding Tar Ebon?" She asked mostly to make it look like she didn't care what Kyra was up to and that their shared glance had been a coincidence. She knew what Isabelle's answer would be.

The girl met her gaze anyway, confusion flashing for a moment before her passive mask resumed its place. "It's loud, crowded and stinky."

"So you hate it?"

Isabelle smirked. "I would if I didn't have friends to care about. And magic."

Emma couldn't help but smile. She had made a difference in someone's life.

The door opened and Kylie emerged, smiling while holding the pretty green dress she'd chosen. "Ready?"

"Let's get back to the Tower before the snow ruins our dresses," Emma suggested.

"Hand them to me," Isabelle said. Emma and Kylie surrendered their dresses to her. Moments later she and the dresses faded to shadow.

"Neat trick," Kylie commented.

"You don't know the half of it." She had regaled part of the story of their first journey into the shadow realm to Kylie upon their safe return, so in fact Kylie did know, but it was the first time she had seen Isabelle using her power. Emma knew the shifter would return in a few minutes, so she pointedly did *not* look inside the tailor's shop this time. Instead she focused on the blacksmith's shop down the street. Smoke billowed out from the chimney at the top and the distant clang of metal on metal echoed through the closed door. It was not an open-air smithy like some of the others in town, which told Emma that he specialized in weapons or armor - high temperature items which needed an enclosed building to forge successfully. Open-air smithies, her mother had told her, were fine for fixing horse shoes or making basic tools or things like nails, but when it came to forging high quality products an enclosed building was necessary to minimize heat loss. Emma didn't share those thoughts with Kylie, for she knew it would likely bore her friend.

Isabelle appeared then, empty-handed, to interrupt her thoughts. "There, safe and sound on your beds."

"Thank you," Emma said, grateful for her friend saving them a trip back to the Tower. "Aren't you afraid of being seen, though?"

Isabelle shrugged. "I don't care. Mundanes will probably just think it's a something all mages can do, and mages will probably just assume it's a new form of magic."

"Which it is," Kylie said. "That's not something *any* mage can do. You're unique in the world, having magic *and* your shifting ability."

"The world is a big place," Isabelle countered. "There could be more like me out there."

"What does your dad say about the probability of that?" Emma asked, more out of curiosity than to challenge her friend's statement.

Isabelle frowned. "I never asked. But it's probably low. He would also say we don't have enough evidence and probably refuse to answer. He's always been logical like that. You ask him what he thinks the weather will be tomorrow and he won't answer until he's analyzed the sky for twenty minutes."

Emma's reply was forestalled by a surge of magic coming from the direction of the harbor. Her eyes went wide. For them to feel it from that distance. "Do you guys feel that?"

Isabelle nodded, looking calm, almost bored, while Kylie's face mimicked what Emma assumed her own face looked like. "Want me to shift us?"

"Yes."

Isabelle wasted no time thrusting out her hands for the girls to take. Once physical contact was made, the world shifted from color to the gray of the shadow realm. In the blink of an eye they were at the end of the street, then another flash brought them to the mouth of the harbor. Emma couldn't sense where the magic had come from within the shadow realm, but an instant later the world returned to color as Isabelle returned them to the physical realm.

Emma groaned at the sight. Her brother, Richard and Cadmon faced off against three other young men. Magic crackled around them as if each side were preparing to unleash hell. Mundanes ran away from the scene of the fight. *What caused the surge of magic?* Then she saw it. A wide circle of charred ground between the two groups of boys. They already begun the fight and were now at a standoff. She ran forward and stopped at the edge of the charred ground, feeling the heat radiating from the stone. If that had been wood, it would have started a fire on the docks. "What the hell is going on?" she demanded. A glance back showed Kylie and Isabelle hanging back. What were they waiting for?

"He started it," Ethan and the boy in the center of the other group said in unison, pointing at each other.

"I don't care who started it," Emma snapped. "Why are you fighting?"

"So, you need a girl to protect you?" the center boy mocked.

Magic flared around Ethan and lightning crackled between his fingers.

"Stop!" Emma ordered her brother before rounding on the other boy. "Who are you?"

"The name's Aurelius." He tilted his head up, as if expecting someone to paint his picture and get his "good side." "We're of House Longclaw.

Emma groaned. Of course the guy picking a fight with her brother would belong to *her* house. "Well, Aurelius, I may be a girl but I can still kick your ass. So run along before you get hurt."

"Oooh," his two cronies said mockingly, while Aurelius threw back his head and emitted a belly laugh. "You're new here," he began after composing himself, "so I'll explain this nicely for you. I'm a seventh-year student. You're not. I get what I want. And right now I want his money pouch."

Emma folded her arms below her breasts. "You mean you want to rob him. I believe theft is illegal, even for mages."

Aurelius smirked. "My father has connections. No charges would stick against me."

"If your father has so many connections, why are you robbing your fellow students? Doesn't Daddy give you enough of a stipend?"

"It's a power thing," Isabelle chimed in, coming to stand next to Emma with Kylie in tow. "I've seen his kind all over the world. My mother eats people like him for breakfast."

"Well, your mother isn't here, sea bitch," Aurelius said, undeterred.

"No," Isabelle agreed, "but I am." She faded to shadow and a moment later appeared behind him, a dagger at his throat. "And I am very lethal."

Where did the dagger come from? Emma wondered. She hadn't seen it on Isabelle's belt. Oh well, a question for another time.

Magic swirled around Aurelius' cronies but they held their attacks, likely waiting for orders from their head man.

"You...wouldn't...," Aurelius managed to say despite Isabelle's knife at his throat.

"Just give me a reason." The girl pulled him closer and pressed the knife further. A trickle of blood ran from the site of the cut.

"What do you want us to do, boss?" the first crony asked hesitantly. He formed a fire ball while his companion formed a frost orb.

Aurelius struggled in Isabelle's grasp. Emma imagined various calculations going through the boy's head. If he backed down he would lose face in front of his cronies and surrender power. If he didn't back down, he risked injury or death. But would Isabelle actually do it? Emma didn't think she'd ever killed anyone. Emma had, and the memory still gave her nightmares. Maybe he was calling her bluff.

I have to do something to help her. "Are a few coins worth dying over?" Emma called. "Her mother is an assassin. How many people do you think her daughter has killed? Do you really want to find out?" *That's the best I've got. I hope it works.*

The boy's eyes opened wide as the implication of Emma's words hit him. "N...no...I guess not," he stammered. "Let me go and we'll leave," he promised.

Emma shared a look with Isabelle. *Do you trust him?* She asked silently. They didn't have a connection between their implants, but she hoped her eyes could convey the meaning.

Isabelle nodded slowly before releasing her grip on him and withdrawing the knife. She shoved him into one of his followers and backed up toward Emma while her knife disappeared to who knew where. "You're lucky. Now go on, get out of here," she ordered sternly. She had a long way to go before her voice would hold the same level of malice and command as her mother's, but it was a start.

Aurelius disentangled himself from his friend and smoothed his clothes, trying to reclaim some small piece of his dignity. "Let's go," he ordered before turning and striding pompously away from the fight.

"Yeah, you run," Ethan shouted after them.

"Run back to your daddy, scum bags," Cadmon added.

Emma sighed. They'd just scared away the bully and already they were taunting him. She held her breath, hoping Aurelius wouldn't turn around to restart the fight. She waited until they were out of ear shot before stalking up to her brother. "What the hell were you thinking?" She shoved her finger at the center of his chest. "Starting a fight in the middle of the harbor? Your magic could have gone out of control. There are wooden ships all around!"

"He's a bully, Emma," Ethan protested. "He wanted to take our money."

"It's just money," Emma said through gritted teeth. "It wasn't worth risking death or injury over."

"Then why did Isabelle defend us with threats of death and injury?"

"She was cleaning up your mess. Isn't that right, Isabelle?"

Her friend walked up beside her and nodded. "I had to de-escalate the situation as it had progressed beyond the point of peaceful resolution, even if you'd given them the money. They were out for blood by that point. My mother would say it was a case where force was necessary."

"Your mother may be a little biased," Ethan said. "Being an assassin and all."

"*Former* assassin," Isabelle connected.

"Once an assassin always an assassin," he said, shrugging.

"You want to repeat that?" Isabelle drew her dagger again.

Emma rolled her eyes. "He's just being an idiot. He doesn't mean anything by it."

Isabelle harrumphed, then gritted her teeth and stalked away. "You can find your own way back to the Tower." She strode past Kylie before shifting and disappearing.

Emma sighed. "You really stepped in it now, Ethan."

"Yeah, our ride just walked away," Cadmon admonished. He shrugged languidly. "You guys want to grab some peppermint beer before heading back?"

Ordinarily, Emma would have declined. She wanted to talk to her friend and make amends. But it was probably a good thing to give Isabelle time to cool down. "Sure, why not?" She looked around, noticing their surroundings for the first time. The activity at the harbor had not slowed despite the snow. Men, and a few women, still strode to and fro with purpose. In the distance, toward the mouth of the harbor, a line of ships sailed in. Her eyes narrowed. That seemed odd to her, but she didn't know much about maritime affairs. Another reason she wished Isabelle were there.

The boys took off toward a nearby tavern with Kylie in tow. Emma followed, catching up with her friend.

"I'm sorry I didn't help," Kylie said softly as they walked.

Emma nodded. "It's fine. There wasn't much you could have done unless a fight broke out. And that would have been disastrous."

"Will Isabelle be okay?"

"I really hope so," Emma said, thinking of her friend.

Chapter 15

Returning to the Tower, Emma sought out Isabelle, but she wasn't in her room or in the common area. She checked the dining hall and mageball arena but finally found her in the library, which was honestly the last place Emma had expected to find the girl. She was reading a book called "Chemistry and Me: A Guide to Human Body Functions."

Emma approached cautiously, not sure how her friend would react. "Hello," she said after Isabelle looked up and didn't immediately shout at her or ask her to leave.

Isabelle sighed. "Hello."

"Can I sit?"

Her friend hesitated for a moment before gesturing to the chair across from her. "Be my guest."

Emma took a seat and sat in awkward silence for at least a minute while Isabelle returned to reading the book. At last, she couldn't take it anymore. "I'm sorry."

"For what?" Isabelle asked.

Was this a test? She had to know what Emma was apologizing for, didn't she? "For standing up for Ethan even after he offended you." She still didn't completely understand why Isabelle had acted the way she did. "I didn't realize it would hurt your feelings so much."

Isabelle pursed her lips and didn't speak for several seconds. "I overreacted," she acknowledged at last, not meeting Emma's eyes. "You don't know how many times a day people say something about my mother. 'Oh, your mother is the assassin?' 'Oh, *Bridgette* is your mother? I'm sorry.' The worst things aren't the comments, though. It's the looks I get. The looks of fear or apprehension. They look at me as if

I were a wild animal that could bite them at any time. It makes me feel like I'll never get out from under the shadow of my mother."

"I'm sorry, I didn't know," Emma admitted. That wasn't strictly true. She knew Isabelle had struggled a little these last few months, but perhaps her joy at learning to shift and mastering that skill had overshadowed the experiences she was recounting to Emma and hid them.

Isabelle shrugged. "It doesn't matter." She continued to read her book, refusing to make eye contact.

"Yes it does matter," Emma insisted. "You're my friend. I don't want you to be hurting, physically or emotionally. What can I do to help?"

"You're already helping," her friend replied, meeting Emma's eyes at last. "Just be here to listen to me. That is the best way you can help."

Emma smiled. "Deal." She hesitated. "Are you sure you don't want to go to the dance tonight?"

Isabelle snorted. "You know dances aren't for me. Besides, I don't have a dress."

"You can't use that excuse. You could shift down to the tailor's shop and be back with a dress in an hour if you wanted." She maintained her smile in an effort to show her friend that she meant nothing hurtful by her comment.

Isabelle chuckled. "You're persistent."

"I'm just being a good friend."

"Do you have a date for the dance?"

Emma shook her head. "No, and I don't need one."

"Now who's being stubborn? Why don't you ask Richard? Or Cadmon?" A teasing tone had entered her voice.

"Ugh," Emma said. "No thank you. Yeah, Richard is cute but...can you imagine how much Ethan would tease me if I went to the dance with his best friend? And don't even go there with that weasel Cadmon. He's slicker than pig grease and probably already has a dozen dates lined up."

"You underestimate him. I'm guessing two dozen dates."

The girls shared a laugh at the mental image.

HOURS LATER, AFTER dressing and doing her hair and makeup, Emma entered the Great Hall and found the music had begun but the dancing itself hadn't started yet. The boys and girls faced one another, their backs pressed against opposing walls, each side too scared to make the first move. Between them the professors stood at intervals like sentinels to ensure the students behaved themselves.

Emma groaned inwardly. It was going to be a long night if no one danced. What about the couples that had come together? She sought out Samira, whom she knew had been coming with Jade, but found the two staring lovingly at one another from across the divide. Even couples were too afraid to go out on the dance floor?

Throat-clearing caught her attention and she looked toward the head of the great hall, where Alivia stood. "Welcome to the twelfth annual snow festival dance. I encourage the students to have fun and enjoy themselves but know that any...overly enthusiastic...touching will result in one of the professors intervening. Magic is strictly forbidden on the dance floor and so are late night rendezvous. Curfew has been extended by two extra hours, but that does not mean you can go roaming the Tower or the town. I know I am talking to children and teenagers but...be careful and use common sense." She paused for response.

The last sentence brought titters from some students, while others cheered.

Alivia smiled at the reaction and lifted her hands. "Let the dance commence!"

Emma's realized her assumption had been wrong. The couples had been purposely separated and now that the dance had begun they joined one another on the dance floor. Some of the younger girls and boys remained stuck to the wall, however. Emma smiled at that. She wished *she* could stand against the wall like that and fade into the background.

She sought out people she knew and found Kylie being pulled out onto the dance floor by Cadmon while Ethan egged them on. Richard looked like a lump on a log in his dress robes, hunched over in his chair with a mug of something in front of him. Emma took a deep breath and walked over to their table. "You guys didn't find any dates?"

Ethan shrugged, swaying to the music. "I'm keeping my options open."

"Meaning every girl turned you down?"

"He asked seven girls on his floor to the dance," Richard chimed in. "They all declined, some more gracefully than others."

As if on cue, Ethan rubbed a red mark on his cheek. "Shut up."

Emma suppressed a girlish giggle, then sobered as she caught sight of Kyra across the fast-filling dance floor. She knew the girl would be there, she'd been shopping for a dress earlier that day, but actually seeing her made her blood boil. *Calm down*, she told herself. *You can't start a fight on the dance floor. What would Alivia think?* She took a deep breath to calm herself but still resolved to keep an eye on the girl.

Her concentration was broken a minute later when a nervous looking boy Emma didn't recognize approached her and bowed. "M'lady, might I have this dance?" He held out his hand expectantly, a smile somewhere between nervous and confident plastered on his face. He wore a formal tuxedo instead of mere dress robes, which Emma considered a point in his favor.

"I would love to dance," Emma said, not really meaning it. She took his hand and rose, allowing herself to be lead onto the dance floor. Once there, she asked, "What is your name?"

"My name is Frederik," the boy replied. Surprisingly, he led her in the dance. But then, he probably had practiced it in past years, while this dance was unfamiliar to Emma. Her experience growing up in Ironforge hadn't offered the opportunity to learn many new dance moves and the ones she did know were far too common for a place like this.

"Oh. I haven't seen you around." That wasn't saying much. She'd been at the Tower less than six months and in truth rarely got to meet more than a few handfuls of different students.

"I'm from House Skycrest. The weather house," he explained when he saw her blank expression.

"Ohhh," Emma said, wracking her brain. She couldn't remember meeting anyone from House Skycrest before. "Well, it's nice to meet you. Is your house a small one?"

He shrugged. "Somewhat. Arch Mage O'Leary is a member though, so we do have some prestige."

"I figured anyone with the nickname 'Lightning O'Leary' would be a member of that house," Emma agreed.

As they danced and traded small talk, Emma kept her eyes on Kyra, who chatted with two of her friends at her table. *Why isn't she dancing?* She had purchased a dress, which suggested she planned on showing it off on the dance floor. Three dances later the fires of suspicion were fed as Kyra rose, left her friends behind and departed the great hall. Emma's eyes narrowed. *Where is she going?* She was forced to wait until the dance was finished to disengage from Frederik. She offered a half-hearted thanks before racing out of the Great Hall. She didn't dare stop to tell her friends where she was going.

Out in the hallway, she glimpsed the elevator door clicking closed. She looked at the numbers on the wall and saw the B-1 icon light up, then B-2, then B-3. *She's going into the basement.* It stopped at B-3. Emma knew that B-4 and beyond were inaccessible to students, though she didn't know why. Instead of taking the elevator, she went to the stairwell and descended. A minute later she cracked open the door to B-3 and peered out. There was no sign of Kyra, and the icon beside the elevator already showed it rising to B-2 and a moment later B-1. A single hallway led away from the elevator.

She crept down the hall, listening for the slightest sound and keeping her magical senses open. A dull magic pulsed in the distance, coming closer as she walked. Halfway down the hall, she froze, hearing voices ahead and to the right. Peaking around the corner, Emma saw the edge of Kyra's dress and moved her head no further.

"...nears," a male voice was saying. "Are you and your followers ready?"

"Yes," Kyra said, sounding confident. "All is prepared."

"Good. Wait for the signal. You will know when it is time. It will not be long."

"Of course, my master." Her dress crept across the floor, suggesting she had curtsied.

Emma panicked. If she exited and found her...what would she do? Instead of turning back, she raced across the doorway and went further into the darkness. She had to find another door, a turn in the hall, something. After several steps she came to a door and tried the knob. It wouldn't budge. Panic rising, she continued down the hall and finally saw a corner. She raced around it and stopped, breathing heavy.

Footsteps sounded from the way she had come, but they became more distant. When she dared to peak around the corner she saw Kyra's retreating back. She waited until the girl had entered the elevator and the doors had closed before emerging from the cross-hall and walking toward the elevator. She stopped along the way and peered into the chamber Kyra had been in. Unsurprisingly, it was empty. What had Kyra used to communicate with her master?

What would Alivia say when she told her? She had to tell her now, there was no uncertainty in her mind that Kyra was a traitor. Heck, she should have confronted her when she exited the room, tried taking her by surprise, but she'd been afraid of facing the possibly more powerful and skilled girl. She again took the stairs to the main level and paused.

Would Alivia be in the great hall, or was she in her offices? *I'll check the great hall first, then go up to her office.* Finding her mentor was of critical importance.

She had barely taken two steps when an alarm sounded, echoing through the Tower and overwhelming every other sound, even the music that had echoed from the great hall. She didn't need magic to know what was happening. The Tower was under attack.

Chapter 16

"Tar Ebon is under attack," a dull, mechanical voice reminiscent of Shadow bellowed after the alarms had finished sounding. "Initiate emergency lock-down procedures immediately."

At first, nothing happened. Emma wracked her brain, thinking what to do now. Did she return to her dormitory, like the emergency procedure called for, or did she continue trying to find Alivia and warn her. Her decision-making process was interrupted as the door to the great hall burst open and hundreds of students and staff burst out. Many of the students ran for the elevator or the stairs, while the professors moved at a brisk walk. It wouldn't be dignified for the professors to be seen running.

Alivia's voice sounded this time, echoing throughout the Tower. "All arch mages are to report to rendezvous point alpha. All mages and senior students are to report to rendezvous point bravo. All students are to return to their dormitories with all haste and prepare defensive spells."

From what Emma remembered of the emergency plan, point alpha was located outside of the Tower, in the courtyard, while point bravo was on the first floor of the Tower, where Emma now stood. She hesitated, wondering if she could remain there and join bravo team, but she dismissed the thought a moment later. They would know in a second that she didn't belong there, no matter how skilled or powerful she was. But she was damned if she was going to return to House Longclaw and wait to be attacked.

I have to find my friends, she thought urgently. Shadow, can you contact Ethan?

I am attempting to reach his implant now, m'lady, Shadow responded. Please wait.

Not that I have anything better to do, she thought, trying to infuse sarcasm into her thoughts. She tapped her foot and watched the students continue to stream out of the great hall, while many professors and what looked like full mages or older students descended and gathered right in front of her or went out the front doors.

Emma didn't sense any magic yet, other than what always drifted around the Tower. Where were the attacks coming from?

A familiar face caught her eye. Professor Quaith was approaching her. He gave her a nod and went straight to the stairs. He chose to descend them. Emma scrunched her face up, wondering where he was going. Was he going to defend the shadow core Emma had seen in the basement or something else? She put it out of her mind as Shadow responded to her.

I have reached your brother, her implant informed her. Connecting now.

The sense that she now shared her mind with someone else fell over her and she thought into the silence. *Hello?*

Hey, where did you go? Ethan asked. One second you were there, the next you were gone.

It's a long story. Where are you?

Still in the great hall, waiting for you. Richard and Kylie are with me. I don't know where Cadmon went.

I'm out in the entryway, Emma responded. *Stay there, I'm on my way.* Without waiting for confirmation, she pushed through the trickle of students fleeing the great hall and entered to find a barren wasteland. Streamers lay on the floor, mingled with food and drink while tables and chairs lay upended. Emma had no illusions that most dances probably ended similar to this, only without the upended tables and chairs that were the hallmark of panicked students doing what they did best.

She spotted her brother then and ran over to the group. She embraced her brother and Kylie and nodded bravely to Richard.

For his part, Ethan looked like he was trying to keep himself held together. Richard looked stoic as usual. Did anything bother him? Even being threatened with death by Bloodcloaks had barely fazed him. Kylie though, she had tearstains littering her face and her makeup was smudged. The smile of relief on her face upon seeing Emma warmed Emma's heart.

"Now are you ready to tell me where you were?" Ethan asked.

"I was in the basement," Emma responded. She took a deep breath and launched into her story. "I followed Kyra and..."

When she was done even Ethan was struck speechless for several long moments. At last he swallowed and offered what he probably thought was a reassuring smile. "At least you survived."

"Yes," Emma snapped. "But Kyra is a traitor. We have to warn someone."

"Well there's an entryway full of mages you could tell," Richard suggested.

Emma shook her head. "They have their orders. I need to tell Alivia, so she can coordinate a defense."

"Telling any full mage is better than telling no one though, isn't it?" Kylie asked.

"No, we have to take care of this ourselves. We have to stop her. But first we have to find Isabelle."

"She's probably upstairs, right?"

"She could be anywhere, with her shifting ability."

"Can you use this," Ethan tapped his head, "to contact her?"

"I've never tried." Emma frowned. "Give me a minute." She concentrated and pulled up the interface to Shadow. *Shadow, can you reach out to Isabelle's implant?*

I'm afraid not. I do not have her unique identifier.

Well, how many people with implants are in the Tower? There can't be that many.

Regardless of the number, without her identifier I cannot contact her.

Could you do a...broadcast? Like how Alivia sent her voice throughout the Tower. Could you send a message to anyone with implants in or around the Tower?

Shadow was silent for a long moment. So long that Emma feared he wouldn't answer. Then, *yes, we could do a wide-band broadcast, boosted by the antenna within the Tower. However, we run the risk of anyone with implants receiving the message, which could reveal our plans.*

It's a risk we have to take. I need my friend.

So be it. Emma got the distinct sense that Shadow was irritated with her. *What shall I broadcast?*

Say this: "Isabelle, we are in the great hall. Join us there."

I am transmitting via wide-band frequency now. Standby.

Indeed, a moment later Emma "heard" her own voice echoing back to her as the signal went out. Any fears that someone nefarious would hear her message did not enter her mind and she crossed her fingers that Isabelle would hear her.

Her thoughts were put to rest a moment later when Isabelle materialized before her. She had changed her outfit, too, now wearing a leather outfit that reminded Emma of an assassin along with a black hooded cloak. She held two daggers in her hand and lifted them as if readying for a fight. She lowered them as her eyes alighted upon Emma. "Emma. I was worried it was a trap."

Emma furrowed her eyebrows. "Who else could transmit to implants?"

"The Cult of Rae has been known to have accessed the network from time-to-time illegally. Or so Mother says."

"Well, I don't have time to worry about the Cult of Rae. In fact, if they want to come at us right now I would be happy to torch them."

Isabelle smiled. "That's the spirit." She sobered. "So what are we doing here, anyway?"

Emma recounted her story again for Isabelle's benefit, but her friend's reaction was different.

"Well, what are we waiting for? Let's get down there before it's too late. Did you track Kyra?"

"No, she took the elevator and by the time I got to the main floor by the stairs she was nowhere in sight. She could have gone to any floor, really. Did you see her up on our floor?"

"No, that snake didn't show her face in the dorm - I would have remembered."

"She had to have gone somewhere," Emma said. "Unless..." her eyes opened wide in horror. "Unless she *knew* I was listening..."

"...and tricked you into leaving that level," Isabelle finished, her eyes grim. "That does sound like something she could do."

"I knew I made too much noise for her not to notice me," Emma chastised herself, smacking her forehead. "To the basement, then."

"Where is Cadmon?" Isabelle asked. "Not that I like the little rat."

"He ran off before the alarm went off," Ethan said. He shrugged. "He's always been a little bit of a coward, ya know?"

"Yes," Emma said dryly. "We know." A through struck her. "You don't think he...?" she pointed toward the floor.

"Is six feet under?" Ethan asked. "Na, he's a survivor."

"No, you idiot," Emma scolded. "Do you think he could be in on this with Kyra?"

"Let's not jump to conclusions," Richard said, always the logical member of Ethan's trio. "He could have sequestered himself with a girl or something for all we know."

"I doubt any girl would be making out with Cadmon," Emma said.

"We can debate who is a traitor and who is just a horny boy later," Isabelle interrupted. "Let's go." Without waiting for anyone, Isabelle started walking toward the entrance.

"Wait," Emma said. "Can you shift us into the basement?"

"No. There's some kind of..." she struggled to find the words to use, "barrier stopping me from accessing the basement from the shadow realm."

"That sounds ominous." And it doesn't bode well for our getting out if things go bad, she thought.

"Ominous or not, we don't have a choice," Isabelle replied bravely.

Together, the four companions exited the great hall and went to the stairs. Students were still clustered in front of the elevator, waiting to go up to their dorms. The mages and older students were still gathered, but one of the arch mages stood there, issuing instructions to them.

Emma paused, considering approaching the arch mage to inform him of the treachery she suspected in the basement. But Isabelle's tug on her arm dissuaded her.

They descended the stairs and came out again on level B-3. "This is where she was communicating with someone," Emma reminded them.

"Yeah, but the shadow core was on level B-5," Isabelle said.

"True." Indeed, they had taken the elevator to B-3 and then the stairs down to the floor they'd cleaned months ago after the failed duel with Kyra. "Okay, let's go down," she said, feeling convicted.

Down they went, deeper into the bowels of the Tower. The distant hum of the shadow generator seemed to be muffled now, replaced with a sense of magic. Magic generated by humans. *This won't be good*, Emma thought. They emerged on their chosen floor and passed several rooms filled with books. They came to the office of Professor McGarvon and Isabelle shoved Emma back before she could shadow the doorway.

"You don't want to go in there," Isabelle said grimly.

"Why not?" Emma asked, a sinking feeling consuming her stomach.

"She's dead. Professor McGarvon is dead."

Now that they'd stopped, Emma could smell burnt flesh. That, coupled with what Isabelle had told her caused her stomach to heave. "Why?" Why had they killed a poor old woman who was just minding her own business? *Why do the cultists do anything? They're monsters. They don't need a reason.*

Isabelle echoed her thoughts. "They have no regard for life. They probably figured she would raise the alarm if she saw what they were doing down here."

"She wouldn't have pulled her nose out of her books and artifacts long enough to raise the alarm, though," Emma protested. "She didn't have to die."

"Life isn't fair," Isabelle said, as if quoting someone, probably her mother. "Now pick yourself back up and let's go. And don't look," she scolded in advance. Then she passed the doorway.

Emma looked at the floor and pointedly did *not* look inside the office. She didn't look back to see whether Ethan or Richard did, but a retching noise followed by a splash suggested one of them had. A glance back showed Ethan wiping his mouth, face pale. *Idiot*, she thought. *He just had to look.* She didn't blame him for puking, she would have likely done the same. She blamed him for looking. *At least he had the courage to look*, a voice said. It wasn't a foreign voice, nor was it Shadow. Just the cynical part of her brain.

They made their way past the bathroom where Emma had first heard Kyra talking to someone, then past the library she and Isabelle had spent a day cleaning. In fact, they had cleaned most of these rooms while serving their detention sentence. They came to a crossroad in the hallway, the one where the bathroom lay at one end and the door to the shadow generator lay at the other end. She braced herself for what she suspected would be there. There had been two guards there previously...

She waited while Isabelle again checked around the corner. The girl sighed. "Two bodies."

Emma nodded, steeling her stomach this time around. She hadn't been prepared for the death of a kindly old woman. She was prepared for two guards, soldiers in the war against the Cult of Rae, dying to protect an important area of the Tower. "I'm ready."

"Not that you have a choice," Isabelle remarked. "We can't turn back now." She turned the corner and led them toward the open door to the shadow generator.

Emma looked straight ahead, focusing on the back of Isabelle's head as she walked. *Don't look down, don't look down,* she ordered herself over and over. They passed into the chamber beyond and stopped, again.

Beyond the guarded door sat a tiny room with another door. They paused in the miniature hallway and looked through the second door. A massive chamber opened up. It was circular and stretched high above them. Was this below the Tower or was it below the Tower courtyard? At the center of the chamber a pillar of purplish-black light spanned from the floor to the ceiling, enclosed by glass.

Eight figures stood in front of the pillar, with seven of them forming a star-shape around a tall figure standing at the center of the design.

"What is that?" Emma whispered.

"A ritual of some sort," Isabelle answered. "Don't you feel the flows of power?"

Emma, having been so riled up by the sight, or thought, of dead bodies and the thrill of possible impending battle, had not been sensing magic actively. She calmed her breathing and stretched out her mind, seeking the magic Isabelle referred to. She felt it after a moment, a surge so great that she kicked herself mentally for not sensing it sooner. *Why isn't the entire Tower down here? The amount of magic they're channeling is massive!*

I suspect, Shadow interjected, that the attack on the Tower and city of Tar Ebon is a distraction meant to hide the activity here.

Shit, you're right, Emma realized. "The attack. It's a distraction."

Isabelle nodded. "I figured that out as well. Also, this chamber is shielded, even more than the rest of the basement level. It's like...," she closed her eyes, "there's a barrier around this chamber and then another barrier around the basement. But...there's no barrier against shifting in this chamber." Her voice held awe.

"So does that mean you can shift out and get help?" Emma pressed, hope rising in her.

"I can try. But what about them?" She pointed to the cultists.

"I don't know if we can fight them alone," Emma admitted. "We need reinforcements. You have to at least try."

Isabelle took a deep breath before nodding. "You're right. Here goes nothing." She faded to shadowy mist and disappeared.

Emma held her breath, hoping for success.

Her hopes were dashed a moment later, when Isabelle re-appeared, shaking her head. "I can't get through that," she pointed over their shoulders. "That interior barrier isolates me from the upper levels of the Tower. It's strange."

"Uh, guys, look," Ethan said, pointing behind the girls, toward the cultists.

Emma whipped her head around and finally saw what the cultists were up to. An inky darkness floated above the central man, who held his hands raised as if holding a goblet aloft. "What is that?"

"A portal?" Isabelle wondered aloud. "But where..." her eyes widened. "A portal to the shadow realm."

"I thought you said you couldn't shift anywhere from in here. That you couldn't reach anywhere."

"I couldn't. But that," she pointed, "must be like...tunneling through the barrier. It's like a gate."

"If that's a gate," Ethan began, "what's going to come through it?"

Chapter 17

The answer to Ethan's question came a moment later as men and women in black robes and soldiers wearing red cloaks stepped through the gateway. Emma stifled the gasp. Yes, she had known these were cultists, but some part of her had still believed it might have been a misunderstanding - a miscommunication of sorts. The sight of an evil army emerging in the bowels of the Tower dispelled any notion to the contrary from her mind.

"We have to get reinforcements," Richard urged from the back of the group. "We cannot hope to fight them on our own."

Emma agreed, but hesitated. If she sent one of the others to run for help they would be down a mage. Being down a mage when there were only five of them could spell disaster for the remaining four. "We can't spare anyone to run and get help," she said, vocalizing her thoughts.

"And I can't shift out of this chamber," Isabelle pointed out again. "We don't exactly have a choice."

Emma thought hard. She could feel the energy of the shadow generator pulsing from beyond the glass enclosure. So much power. If the cultists managed to breach containment and harness that power...she froze. "That's it," she said.

"What's it?" Ethan asked, looking around.

"*We* harness the shadow generator's power to deny them the power. Drawing on that much power would be bound to get attention, either through alarms or disruption of power distributed throughout the Tower."

"Good point. I know I would be annoyed if I was riding a lift and it stopped in the middle of the ride," Ethan chimed in.

"And you," Emma said, pointing to Isabelle, "can you disrupt the gateway for any length of time?"

Isabelle thought, studying the gateway that was even then pouring enemies into the bowels of the Tower. "I don't know," she said at last. "I can try my best."

"Okay. You'll shift and try to stop the gateway. At least then they won't be able to call on more reinforcements."

"Or escape," Richard said darkly.

Emma nodded, fury building up within her. The enemy was in her Tower preparing to kill or maim dozens or maybe even hundreds of students and professors. They couldn't allow them to leave this chamber alive. She took a deep breath. "We need a plan of attack," she pointed out. Rushing out and throwing the first spells that came to mind would potentially waste the element of surprise.

"I'll be shifting," Isabelle said, "once I'm further in."

"Richard and I will go to the right and focus on the Bloodcloaks," Ethan said.

"But you didn't wear your swords," Emma pointed out.

Ethan shrugged. "If they get close enough we can take their swords and fight them with their own weapons."

"Just be careful. Kylie and I will take the left, then. I'll focus on the shadow generator while Kylie watches my back against the dark mages."

"I should help defend you," Ethan said, apparently changing his mind.

"You will be," Emma pointed out. "You'll be stopping them from running me through with a sword." She hesitated. "But if you see Kylie struggling, assistance would be appreciated. But defensive magic only for now. We just need to hold out until reinforcements arrive. We can't afford to burn ourselves out trying to kill them all or leave ourselves exposed."

The others nodded in understanding.

Emma took a deep breath. It was now or never. Every few seconds more enemies appeared. "Attack," she said quietly and led the way into the chamber.

Stone pillars ringed the room, and two stood directly inside the chamber housing the shadow generator. Emma swerved to the left, hiding behind a pillar. Kylie joined her. Across from them, Ethan and Richard took cover behind the pillar on the right. Isabelle faded to shadowy mist and disappeared.

Here goes nothing, she thought. She opened herself to her magic and felt in great detail the waves of energy pulsing from the generator. Each wave threatened to force her to take a step backward. How were the dark mages standing before such a tidal wave of magic hammering against them? Couldn't they feel the magic? Maybe they could but were trained to ignore it. "Why haven't they harnessed the power from the generator?" she wondered aloud even as she sensed the world around her in incredible detail.

"They don't want to draw attention to themselves," Kylie said. "Not until they're ready." She too had drawn upon her magic, for Emma could feel her magical presence floating beside her.

That made sense. The cultists must have known what Emma knew - as soon as the power went down mages would be sent to investigate. If they came down before the cultists were fully prepared their plans could be foiled. "Better for us," she replied. She stepped to her left so she would have direct line of sight of the generator. Line of sight was not required, she knew, but it helped to direct the flows of magic and she needed all the help she could get.

How could she break the containment field? The waves emanating from the generator seemed like excess magic, like waves of heat emanating from a boiling tea pot. How could she harness the magic within? Could she melt the glass with fire? No, there was no source of heat hot enough to do that unless she wanted to freeze the room. Could lightning pass through the glass and make a connection? It was worth a try. She concentrated on forming lightning. Once she struck, it would be no secret that she was there and the enemy would begin attacking her.

She felt a fireball hurtling toward her and instinctively deflected it. Too late. They knew she was there. She unleashed the lightning, directing it not toward the humans before the generator but above them at the towering glass column containing vast amounts of energy. The lightning struck the glass wall and dissipated. Emma groaned. They had been told that glass was a poor conductor of electricity. *Think, Emma, think*, she berated herself.

A shard of ice lanced toward her, threatening to freeze her skin. Kylie deflected it into the ground, causing the stone several meters in front of them to become chilled.

That's it! Emma thought. She could *freeze* the glass wall. Slow the elements of its existence down to the point where the glass became fragile, like a thin layer of ice atop a lake, and then shatter it. She would have to time the shattering carefully so as to contain the magic that would inevitably come spilling out, but she didn't have time to re-consider. She formed a ball of ice and hurled it toward the wall of the generator. It traveled only a few meters before a fireball slammed into it, sending water raining down from the point of collision to splatter on the ground. Emma ground her teeth in frustration and thought furiously. With that many dark mages it would be impossible for something with a travel time to reach beyond their lines. Lightning could because it was instant.

A memory came to her then. Of a lesson where they learned that elements of existence could be manipulated from afar without throwing projectiles. Projectiles served only to focus the magic, but in theory an enemy could be scorched if the temperature of the air around them rose sharply enough, no fireball needed. *What if I froze the glass from afar? But couldn't the enemy just launch fireballs to re-heat the glass?*

If I may interject, Shadow put in, if the molecules of an object stop completely it will be like freezing the object.

What are molecules?

What you call the elements of existence. It's a simpler way to describe the tiny molecules, atoms and particles that make up matter.

Oh. And how do I slow these molecules?

I do not know. I am only an artificial intelligence, I have no experience with magic.

It's worth a shot, Emma concluded. She stretched her mind and felt her awareness floating over the enemy lines before coming to rest in front of the glass. She concentrated and the glass started to morph. No, the glass didn't morph, her vision of the glass changed. She could see the individual elements of the glass, linked together and vibrating like a tuning fork that had just been struck. They vibrated so quickly! Emma reached out with her mind, visualized as a hand, and poked a cluster of the elements making up the glass. She could "feel" the thrumming of the elements as it vibrated up her arm. *Now, how to slow them?* She tried to grab the elements but her hand was too large. Next, she tried pulling the heat from around the elements, but it proved too exhausting and the elements barely slowed. It would take too much time and energy to lower the temperature to the point where the elements froze due to that.

Finally she placed her hand on the glass and *willed* the vibrations to slow. At first the elements resisted and the vibrating in her arm continued unabated. But she poured more magic into the effort and the representation of her arm in the magical realm glowed as power cascaded into the glass. The elements started to glow a yellowish color. *Slow,* she thought. *Slow.* The vibration lessened. She jerked in shock, but the motion caused the glow to fade and the vibration to increase. She had to keep concentrating.

Distantly, she felt heat increasing near her body. Was the enemy close to her? She dared not look back, though she could distantly sense the magical battle ensuing behind her. *Just hang on*, she thought, not daring to expend the energy to speak to the others in the physical realm.

Turning her attention to the elements constituting the glass, she again channeled power through her metaphysical arm into the latticework that formed the glass. It glowed brighter than before and as she willed it to slow it did. This time, however, she did not let surprise interrupt the flow of magic. She wasn't sure she could muster enough magic to start the process a third time. Magic continued to flow and the elements glowed brighter. The glow spread several meters in every direction. *Slow, slow, slow,* she shouted mentally, urging the elements forming the glass to slow. The vibration in her arm continued to decrease. It was working. At last she could feel no discernible vibration. Studying the elements of the glass she found them completely still. She knew it wouldn't last, though. Now, how to shatter the glass?

Shadow, open a channel to Isabelle, she ordered. Once the chime indicated she was connected, she spoke, *Isabelle, are you there?*

At first only silence met her query. Then her friend responded. *I'm a little busy here. This gateway is strong.* Somehow a sense of struggle flowed through the mental link. *I'm trying to close it but it's resisting me.*

Listen, I need you, Emma interrupted. It wasn't that she didn't care about her friend's plight, but right now there was a more important task. I need you to emerge from the shadow realm and throw something physical at a swath of glass that I've weakened. She felt the strain on her magic as the elements of existence forming the glass threatened to resume their vibration. Please hurry.

How do I know which spot to hit?

Look for my magical signature. You'll know.

Okay, I'm coming out now. A flash in the magical realm showed the figure of Isabelle appearing, forming piece-by-piece as if her body was being created by shadows. Emma watched as she drew a dagger and hurled it as hard as she could toward Emma's magical signature. Emma felt the elements within the iron blade, bound together and vibrating rapidly, as it cut through the air. She shoved the last of her reserves into suppressing the vibration of the glass elements as she watched the knife slam into the glass.

It shattered, the latticework forming the glass enclosure in the area she had weakened coming apart and shattering into millions of individual molecules, as Shadow had called them. Emma let out a mental whoop. *Thank you,* she said.

Wow, was Isabelle's reply before her body faded again to the shadow realm. *Good luck.* The link closed.

M'lady, I am detecting high levels of radiation in the chamber. Even as he spoke, the ambient lights of the chamber flickered and died, though light mattered not in the magical realm.

Emma ignored her assistant, even though a part of her was curious what he meant. She felt a surge of energy striking her mind in the magical realm, swirling around her and filling her with more magic than she'd ever felt before. *I feel so powerful,* she thought. She drank deep, pulling more and more magic into herself. She seemed to grow more aware of her surroundings. Suddenly she could see the elements that made up the air, the walls, the floor and even the bodies of the enemies facing her friends. It would be so easy, she thought, to reach out and shatter the elements making up their bodies, to wipe them from existence. She reached out with her mind, intending to do just that, when a voice intruded into her thoughts. "Emma, you did it. Can you make a shield?"

No, I want to destroy them all, Emma thought. How easy it would be to unravel the shadow gateway, to rip her enemies asunder, to break through the ceiling and the layers of dirt above it and into the courtyard beyond. She had the power, unlimited power.

"Emma," the voice came again, more insistent this time. It sounded like Kylie. *Kylie my friend*, Emma thought distantly. *What could she want?* "Emma, we need a shield, now, they're about to overwhelm us!"

Us? Emma thought. Who was us? Then the memory flashed into her mind. Her twin brother, Ethan, her friends from the Tower. But if she destroyed their enemies, they would be saved. Why make a shield when she could end the source of the threat?

Emma, a male voice intruded into her thoughts. *That isn't the way. What would Mom and Dad say? You'll lose your soul if you go down that path.*

Ethan? Emma thought. It sounded like him. How had he heard her thoughts? *But I can end the threat, right here and now.*

At what cost, Emma, he pressed. *If you do this the darkness will consume you. Don't let the shadow win.*

Emma struggled to see his side of things. Maybe the shadow would win, maybe she would be consumed, but if this was what being consumed felt like, she didn't want to stop. *It feels so...good*, she replied. *The power. It's...awesome.*

I know, Ethan said. *But if you use it to kill it will change you forever. You have to form a shield. Defend us - don't use that magic for revenge. Please. As your brother, I'm asking, no, pleading for you not to do it.*

Emma was tempted to ignore him. To reach out and destroy their enemies anyway. *I'd be doing the right thing*, she told herself. *But you would lose everything*, her own voice said in her head. That caused her to take a mental step back. The power continued to course through her, but the murderous intentions seemed to be fading. He was right. *Okay, I'll make a shield*, she told him, then pulled her magical body back to where her physical one was and started channeling the awesome power flowing through her into shields. Balls of fire, streaks of lightning, shards of ice and more struck the newly made shields with no effect, dissipating into nothingness before fading into the environment. This much power reminded her of the Staff of Agamar, only...stronger. Much stronger. And she would use it to save lives, not take them.

Can you do anything about that shadow gateway? Isabelle chimed in through the implant.

Emma studied it. Destroying, or sealing, that wouldn't cause her to kill outright. But what if people were transiting through the gateway while she closed it? She had no idea whether the transportation would be instantaneous or prolonged. She assumed it was instantaneous, so there would be no risk of anyone being in a tunnel of sorts while she closed down the gateway. *Yes, I can do it*, she thought. Checking her shields one last time, they were holding exceptionally well, she reached out and moved her mind in front of the shadow gate.

The shadow gate seemed to Emma to be a writhing, twisting mass of energy and matter. Elements of existence, some she knew and some she didn't recognize, mingled together. She stared at the heart of the gateway and felt as though she could see through it into the shadow realm. Almost. *Now how to close it*? Could she slow the molecules of the shadow gate like she had the glass? Would that do anything? Emma doubted it.

She studied the way the elements seemed entangled, as if they'd been combined to create something new. *What would happen if I broke apart the entangled elements?* She probed with her magic, feeling at a bundle of two elements. She pressed a single finger to the bundle and felt a vibration like she had with the glass. *I'm not trying to slow them this time*, she thought. *I need to split them.* She focused on that outcome. *Split, split, split.* She imagined the two elements splitting in half, separating. At first, nothing happened. She channeled more magic down her metaphysical arm, feeling the magic from the shadow generator surging through her body and threatening to burst out of her skin. *Just a little longer*, she thought. The magic gathered at her finger-tip and spread like ink in water through the entangled elements, glowing yellow like before. She again exerted her will and this time she felt a tearing sensation and saw with her mind's eye the targeted elements separating but she was momentarily thrown back by a miniature explosion of power from the point of separation. *How did that happen?*

Satisfied at the result, she studied the rest of the gateway. It could have been her imagination, but she could have sworn the structure seemed to wobble. She had destabilized it slightly. *Now to repeat it.* She moved on to the next bundle of entangled elements and plucked them apart. When the expected explosion came she deflected it with a shield and moved on to the next bundle. After that shattered she decided to try multiple bundles at once. She targeted five and in one swift motion split them. A larger explosion flashed outward, absorbed by her shadow generator-enhanced shields, before the entire structure started to unravel. The gateway wobbled noticeably now as its constituent elements shattered of their own volition and moments later blinked out of existence, without the resulting release of energy this time.

Emma pulled her mind back to hover near her body and inspected the shield. It continued to hold, despite repeated barrages from the dark mages. Satisfied, she pulled her mind back enough so that she could interact with the physical realm while continuing to control the elements in the magical realm. "I did it," she said, her voice hoarse.

Beside her, Kylie turned and smiled. "You destroyed the gateway and you're holding back their attacks. We might make it out of this after all."

No sooner had Kylie spoken than the shadow generator blinked out of existence. Emma stared in shock as the flow of power through her body ceased and exhaustion threatened to overwhelm her. She staggered and used the pillar to hold herself up. "No," she exclaimed in shock. What had happened?

I believe it was a safety feature, Shadow chimed in. As I mentioned, the breach in containment unleashed a large amount of radiation. The shadow generator likely shut down to prevent an explosion or intense contamination of the area.

What is radiation?

Radiation is energy traveling through space, Shadow explained. Most radiation, such as sunlight, is harmless over shorter periods of time. However, other radiation, such as what the shadow generator released, is harmful to human tissue.

Meaning it could kill us?

Long-term exposure could, yes.

Oh. The revelation that she could have killed herself and her friends caused her to sag further. She barely noticed the shield falling apart as the high energy surging through it ceased. They were vulnerable once more.

Please let that have been enough time for someone to have noticed. Surely as soon as containment was breached and the power was interrupted someone would have come to investigate. Where were they?

Isabelle appeared beside Emma, startling her. "Now we've done it. They're like cornered rats."

Indeed the dark mages, momentarily distracted by the destruction of their shadow gateway and the destabilization of the shadow generator, turned their attention to Emma and her friends once more. Several Bloodcloak bodies littered the ground between the two groups and even a few dark mages were dead, but there were still too many for the students to fight in their weakened state. They could run, but then everything they'd done would be for naught as the dark mages made their way into the Tower to wreak havoc.

Across from Emma, Ethan and Richard looked worse for wear, with Richard having a bandage around his upper arm and blood streaming down it and Ethan limping as he went to peak around the pillar. Her brother still seemed in good spirits as he gave her a thumbs up.

Emma couldn't help but laugh. Here they were, exhausted and outnumbered and about to die but at least they were giving their lives for something important. Kylie looked askance at her but Isabelle, seemingly understanding the joke, laughed along with her.

The dark mages threw fire, ice, lightning and wind magic in various forms seemingly in unison.

Emma raised a shield once more and felt her friends strengthening it with the remainder of their reserves. Her head pounded and her vision blurred. This was it, one final stand before their defenses crumbled.

Magic surged from behind the students. The barrier, which had barely held against the lightning and would have crumbled against the slower projectiles, glowed bright as dozens of streams of magic flowed toward it, bolstering it.

Emma, straddling the magical and physical realm still, turned and blinked, her entire body aching, to see dozens of mages running into the chamber. A dozen had stopped, their eyes white as they channeled magic into the barrier, but dozens more streamed through, running left or right and taking up positions behind pillars around the room. Magic flared then from their positions but no attacks came. What were they waiting for? Emma sagged in relief and withdrew her power from the barrier. They didn't need her trickle of magic now.

"Do you surrender?" a voice boomed. The speaker, Arch mage O'Leary, revealed herself a moment later, stepping through the doorway and striding between the first two pillars to stand directly behind the barrier. Clearly, she was not afraid.

The cultists ceased their attacks and huddled together, preparing their own barrier, but none spoke. The remaining Bloodcloaks formed ranks in front of them, swords and mundane shields of iron raised as if those could stop magic.

Alivia appeared to sigh before drawing upon her magic. "You have one chance," she informed them. "Surrender now and you will face a tribunal but you will live. Continue to fight and," she gestured behind herself, "you will be destroyed." As if to emphasize her point, all of the mages who had entered the room drew upon their power to the max. Emma wanted to join them but even touching her magic made her head pound. She just wanted to sleep, but she had to see how the stand-off ended.

Some of the dark mages, seemingly the shorter ones, looked behind them toward a group of taller ones at the rear of the formation. Was there some uncertainty among the ranks? The question was answered moments later as six of the cultists near the front moved forward, toward Alivia. "We surrender," a girl's voice said. It sounded familiar, but Emma couldn't place it immediately.

"Get back here, girl," a male voice from the rear snapped. "I will not allow you to do this."

The girl whirled and pulled down her hood. "I didn't sign up for this," she gestured behind her and then up at the shattered shadow generator. "Face it, we've lost."

"Traitors. Kill them," he ordered. The Bloodcloaks rushed forward, intending to impale the defecting dark mages.

Alivia didn't give them a chance. Magic flared and lightning streaked between the defecting dark mages to strike the approaching Bloodcloaks. They jerked for several long seconds before dropping like bags of flour to the stone floor. The remainder of the Bloodcloaks stared in horror before throwing their swords and shields to the ground and following after the defectors.

A dozen dark mages remained, maintaining their barrier as if it could stop dozens of mages. Perhaps it could stop a few attacks, as Emma and her friends had done against their superior numbers, but they wouldn't stop them for long. For several long moments the two groups glared at one another. Then the dark mages withdrew daggers from beneath their cloaks and held them, two-handed, below their rib cages, pointed up toward their hearts. "For the glory of Rae'Shela," the tallest of their number at the rear said, then as one the dozen dark mages thrust upward with their daggers, impaling their hearts.

Chapter 18

Emma gasped in shock. She had expected the cultists to fight to the death, not resort to suicide. She refused to look away, though, as the bodies fell to the floor and blood pooled beneath them. It was over.

"Lower your hoods," Alivia ordered. If she were perturbed by the suicide of a dozen enemy mages she didn't show it.

The six remaining cultists lowered their hoods.

Emma had expected Kyra, but the others. She gasped. "Cadmon?" She shared a glance with Ethan, whose eyes were wide, portraying as much shock as she felt. One of his best friends at school had been a traitor. She didn't recognize the other four cultists, but their younger appearances made it all too obvious they were students at the Tower.

If Alivia was surprised, she showed no hint of it. She merely gestured toward them. "Take them."

A dozen mages stepped forward and dragged the six traitors out of the room. Kyra snarled at Emma as she passed, while Cadmon kept his eyes downcast with the others.

How could he have betrayed us like that? Emma wondered. It didn't make sense, but the evidence was overwhelming.

Alivia approached the cluster of deceased cultists and removed the hood of the one who had spoken. Emma squinted, trying to see who it was. She gasped a moment later, shocked twice within as many minutes. "Professor Quaith?" she said aloud. The pieces clicked in her mind. She had seen him taking the stairs soon after the alarm went off, but she hadn't actually thought anything of it. Had he been the ringleader? Alivia removed the hoods from the other corpses but Emma did not recognize the others, though she heard murmurs emanating from the mages encircling the chamber. Had more of the hooded figures been professors she hadn't met? Or other mages who weren't professors? It sounded likely, as it would have been difficult to infiltrate enough mages into the Tower to begin the ritual that had opened a portal otherwise. "Clean this mess up," Alivia ordered. "Burn the bodies."

Ethan and Richard joined the three girls as Alivia made a bee-line right toward Emma. "Are you all right?" Richard asked, putting a hand on her shoulder and looking into her eyes.

Was he checking for damage? Emma flushed at the feel of his hand on her shoulder. It wasn't intimate by any stretch, but still...maybe it was the exhaustion getting to her. She could barely stand, after all. "I'm just so tired," she said. She suspected he was equally tired.

"What happened?" Alivia demanded as she stopped in front of the group of friends.

Emma took a deep breath. "When the attack commenced we suspected the cultists were going after the shadow generator," she didn't take time to explain how she knew - there would be time for that later. "We came down here to investigate. The cultists had conjured a shadow gateway and were funneling reinforcements into the Tower. There wasn't time to send a warning, so we disabled the shadow generator to warn you."

"*You* disabled the generator?" Alivia asked incredulously. "Not the cultists?"

Emma shook her head. "We would have been torn apart if they had."

"The entire school likely would have been," Alivia confirmed. She sighed. "I'm relieved you survived, though what you did was ill-timed. The Tower will be defenseless until the generator can be restored." She looked to Isabelle. "Can you find your father and bring him here? I believe he is the only experienced engineer left who can make the repairs."

"I can," Isabelle confirmed. "Shall I go now?"

"Yes," Alivia said curtly.

Isabelle turned and jogged into the corridor, heading for the surface. She could shift in the chamber but hadn't been able to find a way *out* of the chamber. Perhaps coming into her power so recently affected what she was capable of? Clearly the cultists had been able to open a portal to the shadow realm despite the barrier surrounding the chamber.

"What happened out there?" Emma asked.

Alivia looked angry all of a sudden, though it did not appear she was angry at Emma. "A well-organized trap," she spat. "Zerrecia played us like a fiddle. He knew exactly where to hit us to distract us the most."

"What happened?" Emma repeated, quieter this time.

The arch mage sighed. "They staged a multi-pronged attack we never saw coming. They infiltrated the harbor using various trade ships while using traitors within the ranks of our own guards to open several of the gates and let an attacking force inside. Meanwhile dissidents within the city started setting fires and tying up the guards near the center of the city. It was clever on Zerrecia's part, even if it was doomed to fail."

Emma stared in horror. "How did they manage to get close to the city walls to charge in?"

"A concealment spell," Emma said. "They concealed themselves by bending light around them and moving very slowly toward the gates. Then, when the attack commenced, the troops ran out from under the concealment as the gates opened. By the time our forces deployed and regained control they had a prolonged fight on their hands. And at the harbor, several ships were burned before the enemy was killed."

"But you said it was doomed to fail?" Obviously, it had failed, if they were standing there to have this conversation.

"Yes. It was a distraction from this," she indicated the chamber behind her. "A calculated sacrifice designed to draw us away from the Tower and allow the cultists time to enter."

"And if they managed to gain a foothold in the Tower, they would have been hard to dislodge," Emma guessed.

"Correct. You saved the Tower, Emma. You and your friends." She smiled tiredly. "Now I want you all to report to the infirmary, including Isabelle when she returns, and get some rest. You, most of all, deserve it. And thank you for your service."

Emma flushed. It felt odd having the arch mage thank her for anything. "Of course. We just did what anyone would do."

Alivia shook her head. "Not everyone would have put their lives on the line like you did. Your parents would be proud."

I'll have to write them a letter, Emma thought. Let them know I'm all right, though I doubt they'll hear about the attack on the Tower for months. "Was Zerrecia involved in the attack? Was he," she looked past Alivia to the pile of corpses, "involved personally in the attack?"

"I wish he had been, so I could have torn him apart. But alas he threw Professor Quaith to the wolves. Perhaps he would have come through the gateway after they'd secured more territory, but we'll never know."

"What if he tries again?"

"We will tighten the defenses." Her face became grim. "And we are going to take the fight to him soon."

Emma shivered at the ice in the mage's tone but nodded. "We will go now." She turned and led her friends out of the room. The corridor was dim, with only a quarter of the lights functioning. Did they have a backup generator somewhere? How else would they maintain *any* power? She would have to ask Alivia, or Isabelle's father, later. Right now she wanted to sleep for a hundred years.

The elevator was disabled, so they climbed the stairs to the floor housing the infirmary and entered, puffing from the exertion. Most of the beds were occupied and healers and servants ran to and fro. One of them stopped and stared at Emma and her friends, perhaps assessing the state of their wounds, if any. She pointed to a line of chairs along the wall behind them. "Sit there and wait to be seen," she snapped.

Emma nodded her understanding. There were more seriously wounded people than her in that place. She turned to do as instructed when her legs gave out and the ground rushed to meet her, darkness enveloping her a moment later.

Chapter 19

Light stabbed into Emma's eyeballs, causing her to squeeze her eyes closed a moment later and groan in discomfort.

"Emma, can you hear me?" a familiar voice came. Alivia sounded like she was sitting right next to her.

Emma nodded. "Yes." Her voice came out raspy, as if her mouth were as dry as sandpaper.

"Can you try opening your eyes again?" Alivia asked. "I've dimmed the lights some."

Complying with Alivia, Emma opened her eyes and forced them to remain open. She glanced to the side, where the familiar smiling face of the arch mage met her. "Hello," she said dully.

"How are you feeling? Any pain or discomfort? Other than the light."

Emma chuckled, then sobered and moved her arms and legs, turned her head from side to side and wiggled her toes. She sat up a moment later, looking around. The infirmary, which had been full when she arrived there, was now virtually devoid of patients. She saw only two students sitting on beds being examined by healers or their staff. "No, no pain," she said. "How long was I unconscious? And where is Ethan and the others?"

"You were unconscious for over a week," Alivia informed her gently. The healers said that on top of almost draining your magic entirely you also had bleeding in your brain."

"Oh," Emma said. Is that true, Shadow?

Quite, m'lady, Shadow responded after an unusual delay. You sustained heavy damage that almost overwhelmed my ability to heal you. Without outside intervention you would have died.

A close call, then, Emma said, feeling like she was pointing out the obvious. She met Alivia's eyes. "Thank you for saving me."

Alivia smiled. "You're the one who saved the Tower. We should all be kneeling to you. As for Ethan and the others, they showed symptoms of magical exhaustion but recovered much faster than you."

Emma pointed slowly to the lights mottling the ceiling. "It looks like the power was restored."

"Yes. It took Jason three days to restore the containment barrier and restart the shadow generator." She paused dramatically. "I actually heard him curse while working on it, and I *never* hear that man curse."

"Probably cursing me," Emma said ruefully. "But everything is back to normal?"

Alivia snorted. "As normal as things can be. We buried the dead and repaired the damage to the city. The cultists were hunted down and captured or killed if they resisted. Few escaped, so I have to believe we made a substantial dent in their numbers."

Kyra, and Professor Quaith, she thought, swallowing hard. "And the students who..." she hesitated, then plunged ahead, "betrayed the Tower?"

Alivia's face mimicked a thundercloud in that moment and it looked as though she could spew lightning from her eyes at any moment. "The traitors," she said, excluding any mention of them being students, "are currently in a cold cell awaiting a tribunal." She shook her head. "I can't believe they betrayed us."

"I think they were led astray by the adults," Emma guessed. "I mean, Professor Quaith and Kyra must have been close."

"That is no excuse." Alivia sounded like she'd heard that excuse many times during the week Emma was reviving. "They were part of something that cost dozens of lives, not just here but across the city. They might not have swung the sword but they certainly didn't stand against it either. Their punishment is not up to me, but if it were I would electrocute them where they stand."

Emma nodded, unable to find words. "Will classes continue?"

"They are canceled for another week, but the students are getting antsy. Just today there were three impromptu duels in the halls. We may need to restore classes sooner than planned to stop a civil war from breaking out among the students."

Emma couldn't help but crack a smile at the mental image which came to mind. The students did like to prank and test their magical prowess against one another.

"Are you going after Valdorf's apprentice?"

"We don't know where he is," Alivia stated flatly. "And with our ranks further diminished we can't spare many mages to go looking for him." Her face contorted in anger again, though Emma suspected it wasn't toward her. "But rest assured, a plan is in the works." She stood. "But enough of that for now. Your friends and brother are eager to see you. The healers had to chase them out of the ward numerous times while you rested. Even now they're barely contained to the waiting room." She headed toward the door to the medical ward. "Continue to rest. No strenuous activity or major magical exertion. Understand?" She presented a mock serious face.

Emma nodded, maintaining the serious tone the conversation had taken. "I understand. And thank you."

Alivia nodded and headed to the door. No sooner had the door closed behind her than it burst open again and her brother, Kylie, Richard and Isabelle stepped in.

Where's Cadmon? Oh, that's right, the memory of seeing him standing behind Kyra hit her. Her memory was still spotty from the time of the battle.

Your brain is still recovering, Shadow said, intruding into her thoughts. *I suspect you will regain full neural and memory functionality within twelve point six hours.*

I can't wait, Emma thought sarcastically. Who knew what horrific memories might surface from the battle?

Ethan was the first to approach, giving her a big hug which caused her to grunt in pain.

"Easy, you oaf," she scolded him once she could breathe again. "I'm better but still fragile."

"Oh, sorry," Ethan said, his face turning red with embarrassment. "My bad."

"How are you coping?"

"With what?" He sounded wary.

"With Cadmon," Emma said, as if it should be obvious. "His betrayal."

Ethan sighed and stared at the floor, hands clenching into fists. "Please don't speak his name again."

"He's written him out of his book of friends," Richard said from near the back of the group. He was tall enough to see over the heads of the girls.

Emma quirked an eyebrow. Did Ethan have enough friends to warrant a *book*? She refrained from asking. Her brother was on the brink, she knew, of exploding in anger. Instead she said, "Okay, I won't." She looked to Isabelle. "You managed to find your father without incident?"

"Yeah, I knew he was with my mother and it was easy to find her. She stands out like a beacon of shadow on the seas. But my father also gave me an amulet of sorts that will let me track him when in the shadow realm, in case he and Mother get separated."

"Smart," Emma said. "Alivia said he repaired the shadow generator in short order?"

Isabelle snorted. "Three days is like a lifetime for my father. He was cursing and even threw some tools. I've never seen him that angry before in my life, even when the ship was almost sinking."

Emma made a mental note to ask Isabelle about a time when her father's ship was almost sinking, then smiled and looked to Kylie. "Are you okay?"

"I've been better," Kylie said. She rubbed the small of her back. "You guys might have those things," she waved vaguely toward Ethan, Emma and Isabelle, "in your blood, but I don't. I had to heal the old-fashioned way."

Be glad you survived at all, Emma thought, though she refrained from sharing her thoughts out loud. Instead she said, "I know how that feels." The memory of recovering after nearly burning to death at her brother's hands still haunted her some nights. She looked last at Richard. "And you?"

Her friend shrugged his bulky shoulders expressively. "I'm tougher than I look. You did all the hard work." The others nodded agreement at his words.

"Yeah, that was awesome," Ethan put in.

"I couldn't have done anything if you guys hadn't held them off long enough," Emma pointed out. "We did it together."

"Yeah, but how cool was drawing on all that power?" Ethan asked.

Emma shrugged. "It reminded me of using the Staff of Agamar, only without the nastier side effects."

"Like death," Isabelle said, deadpan.

"Like death," Emma agreed. She forced a smile. "I'm glad we made it out of this intact. Were the dorms affected at all?"

"You didn't hear?"

"Obviously not, if I'm asking."

"Professor Quaith left nasty traps in our dorms, and so did some of the other traitors on other floors. At least a dozen students died in total from the traps before they were disarmed."

"Oh," Emma sobered. She'd hoped her home away from home had remained intact at least. To hear that it hadn't left her feeling less confident than she had been a minute earlier.

"Don't worry, they swept the floors thoroughly for more traps," Kylie assured her. "We're back in our own beds."

"Did you write to Mom and Dad?"

Ethan nodded. "Yeah, I mailed it out a couple days after the battle. I haven't heard anything from them yet, of course, but I don't expect we will for a few days."

"I could shift there. Maybe," Isabelle amended.

Emma couldn't help but smirk. "That's okay. I don't want you running into Valdorf again."

"Hey, I also found the Halls of Light," Isabelle said, faking an indignant tone. "You know, one of the greatest marvels of our age?"

"How could I forget?" Emma said. She sighed and laid her head back, suddenly exhausted.

"We'll let you get some rest," Ethan said. He touched her shoulder as sleep overtook her.

TWO DAYS LATER EMMA sat with the rest of the houses in the Great Hall. A far more somber tone hung over the room than in previous weeks and months. Instead of merriment, constant conversation and jokes, silence held sway, interspersed with worried whispers.

Alivia stood and all eyes turned to her. She cleared her throat and amplified her voice, though in the silence Emma suspected they could have heard a pin drop. "Today we mourn the loss of many great mages and students, all of whom had many great years ahead of them. Their lives were cut short by the Cult of Rae, a sect of fanatics with no value for human life."

Emma blinked. She knew all this. But judging by the looks on some of the other students, it wasn't necessarily common knowledge.

"We thought them beat," Alivia continued. "We thought them cowed twenty years ago when their leader was defeated. But we were fools. We allowed ourselves to be fooled in our complacency. No more," her voice became firm. "They came here, into our home, thinking us easy prey. They came, expecting us to be destroyed like hens by a fox. But they found no easy prey here, and were destroyed.

"Mark my words. We *will* see the Cult of Rae destroyed. We will crush them as surely as the sun banishes the shadows. The ones responsible for this vicious attack will rue this day. The Tower stands, and may it stand forever more."

"The Tower stands," Emma intoned along with the rest of the students filling the great hall. Tears slid down her cheeks, encompassing her sadness, fear and, most importantly, her anger. They had attacked her home, the place she felt safest outside of Ironforge. They would pay, and she would do whatever necessary to see that they did.

Don't miss out!

Visit the website below and you can sign up to receive emails whenever Dayne Edmondson publishes a new book. There's no charge and no obligation.

https://books2read.com/r/B-A-ZEND-UBCS

BOOKS 2 READ

Connecting independent readers to independent writers.

Did you love *The Cursed Tower*? Then you should read *Halls of Light* by Dayne Edmondson!

The Cult of Rae have been dealt a blow, but they are far from defeated.

Now, as the summer break approaches and Tar Ebon is attacked, Emma embarks on a journey with a new allies.

But things do not go as planned, for the Cult of Rae are back with a plan for ultimate revenge, including bringing back their banished leader and gaining access to weapons that could end the world.

Can Emma and her allies stop the Cult of Rae before they use the Halls of Light to bring about the apocalypse?

The third installment in the Mageborn Saga, "Halls of Light" takes place six months after "The Cursed Tower" and around twenty years after The Shadow Trilogy book "Shadows Fall."

Buy now to jump into the magical adventure.

Read more at https://www.darkstarpublishing.com.

Also by Dayne Edmondson

The Dark Tide Trilogy
Emergence
Eclipse
Ruin

The Mageborn Saga
Mageborn
The Cursed Tower
Halls of Light

The Seven Stars Universe
Ghost Ranger
Space Commando

The Shadow Trilogy
Blood and Shadows
Time of Shadows
Shadows Fall

Standalone
The Complete Dark Tide Trilogy
The Complete Shadow Trilogy

Watch for more at https://www.darkstarpublishing.com.

About the Author

Dayne Edmondson lives in southeastern Michigan with his wife and two young children, a boy and a girl. He writes part time and works a day job.

His books can be read in this order:

The Shadow Trilogy:
1. Blood and Shadows
2. Time of Shadows
3. Shadows Fall

Mageborn Saga:
1. Mageborn
2. The Cursed Tower
3. Halls of Light (coming 2019)

The Seven Stars Universe:
1. Ghost Ranger (coming 2019)

The Dark Tide Trilogy:
1. Emergence
2. Eclipse
3. Ruin

Dayne enjoys reading, writing, the occasional video game, watching TV with his wife, walking and spending time with his children indoors or out.

He writes and reads science fiction and fantasy. Some of his favorite authors/books include Robert Jordan, Brandon Sanderson, (almost) all the Star Wars EU books, Elizabeth Haydon, Christopher Nuttall and more.

Read more at https://www.darkstarpublishing.com.

About the Publisher

Dark Star Publishing is a small-press publisher of science fiction and fantasy novels. They place particular emphasis on books written **in** the Seven Stars Universe (the universe created by author and owner Dayne Edmondson).

For more information, visit https://www.darkstarpublishing.com

www.ingramcontent.com/pod-product-compliance
Lightning Source LLC
Chambersburg PA
CBHW051248250626
47155CB00009B/3213